WE BEAT THE GODS

Saad Quadri

Leadstart
INKSTATE

ISBN 978-93-90040-53-7

First published in India 2021 by Leadstart Inkstate
A Division of One Point Six Technologies Pvt Ltd

Sales Office:
Unit No.25/26, Building No.A/1,
Near Wadala RTO,
Wadala (East), Mumbai – 400037 India
Phone: +91 969933000
Email: info@leadstartcorp.com
www.leadstartcorp.com

Disclaimer: The views expressed in this book are those of the Author and do not pertain to be held by the Publisher.

Editor: Abhishek James Chandran
Cover: Ashwini Jadhav
Layouts: Kshitij Dhawale

To my Mother,
Mercy of Allah

CONTENTS

PROLOGUE

This moment, finally, it's right in front of me. I have found what I was looking for. My nerves demand peace. My heart pumps with authority and with the sound of each beat in my ears I am more focused. With each step I am more certain. I want to ask why you are so sad and I will. Why are you not living your life?

I move calmly and slowly. In next few minutes my nerves are calm, but the guilt took that space. In the darkness of frozen sea, everyone came uninvited to haunt me.

Saadgi tumhari, awaargi hamari
Bad rahi hai

Nikharna tumhara, bikharna hamara
Har ek nazar per

Aahein tumhari, saasein hamari
Sun raha hoon

Maatha tumhara, kahani meri
Likh raha hoon

Tajurba tumhara, hosla hamara
Bad raha hai

Faasla hamara, maashra saara
Jal raha hai

Maatha mera, shikan tumhari
Dikh rahi hai

Akad tumhari, fiqr hamari
Pahad si hai

Mohabbat tumhari, zindagi hamari
Ghat rahi hai

Saadgi hamari, awaargi tumhari
Bad rahi hai

CHAPTER 1

HIS

The bench is facing the sea to embrace the polite view of the sea converging into the sky or diverging into the unknown. Hard to decide but who cares, it looks beautiful. The meeting point of the river and the sea is in anarchy. The sea keeps on pushing itself over the river. The river looks sad and silently snakes itself into the greenery in another direction. I like watching the silence of the river with sound of waves from the sea, a quiet person shouting from inside.

The construction workers must have debated the importance of placing the bench neither too close nor too far from the boundary separating the sea and land. Though it is very unlikely that they gave a second thought what side the bench should face. The importance of the place is the view of the sea and the bench must face towards it. Because of this importance being in its rightful place, I have to turn my neck like a giraffe every time my sixth sense deceives me.

The sea looks like an expanse of open and white ground from distance, smooth. I want to stand at the edge of the sea, at the line that separates Sea and sky, and look back at this place and then take a leap of faith into the unknown like one of those heroes from action movies but it resembles more like a suicide scene to me. Maybe then I will find a new world in the depth of hope or I will find a way through the tunnel that connects the sea and the river underground, the river that looks green, brown and transparent. When I come out from the river travelling through the tunnel that connects them, will I look like green, brown or transparent?

Yet, the closer view will let us know the details of few floating objects and half-drowned things of people. I might find a book sitting at the bottom of the river, waiting for someone to find it. A book that has forgotten all the words written into it or the words sitting so long under water that they learnt how to be transparent like a host. Words have hidden themselves becoming invisible in the book and only a worthy person can read those words, or the book is breathlessly waiting to embrace a new story. Then there will be wooden boats of children half sunk like a person hanging from building, waiting to be rescued. How many dead have floated in this river? How many memories flow in the river? Maybe all these events are chronologically recorded in the book and maybe the book is the heart of the river. How big would the heart of the sea be? I think that is the reason why when the river meets the sea, it becomes calm. There is always someone else stronger than you are or with more pain.

The lives that the river and the sea had drowned in themselves, they did so with no bias on where you were from or what you did. If you are not good enough to be on top of them, you will be beneath them, and then afterwards they will put you on top and show you off around. They give the sense of a tyrant, a bully. Loved ones come to neither avenge the fallen nor hate the unchallenged powerful kings. Yet people visit to enjoy their existence and they flow taking the shape of whatever accommodates them, losing and gaining their recognition. The living and nonliving nature make their souls immortal.

The Bench is cleansed by different seasons, either washed thoroughly or wiped. The status of the wooden plank on the bench is critical with the seasonal renter occupying the other half. The plank is frozen on the iron support of the bench. People have carved "he loves her" on the wooden part and the "he" part has fallen. Could it be dramatically possible that he stopped loving her when the wooden part fell? I wonder if God must have written our names on the wooden slate and hung it up on the wall, that takes beating from different seasons, and the day the wooden slate falls, we fall. After not more than two seasons, the iron skeleton will be left alone, and people will carve "he loves her" on it. Would that make them love each other forever?

The Sun is resting in peace for almost a month now and does not seem to be coming back to life. Birds are shrieking to keep themselves warm. Ice is in no mood to melt and the winds are singing icy cold songs but the mere thought of you coming to this place is enough to keep me warm. Your thoughts gave me anxiety, panic attacks and racing heartbeat decades back. Anyways, time has changed everything.

Even my good morning was very lazy today. I woke up at six sharps with the usual laziness to leave the bed and did not had a heart to take a bath, but I did. Big day after all and one needs to be tidy and fresh for such times. I thought about you, us. About days when we breathed each other. Days, hours, minutes and seconds passed with ease when we were together. When you walk towards me with the same manly walk, chest outwards and hip inwards, what should I say at that moment?

"Hi, how are you doing?"

You will say "fine, thank you. How about you?"

"I am good, thanks for asking."

Wouldn't that be as formal as if meeting some client at work? Can we be comfortable in each other's company like the good old days? Can we jump to the part directly where we can show our love to each other without thinking if it is too early to be so comfortable? Can we ever be the same?

To come to an agreement with myself for bathing now or before I left was an interesting one. My body and mind were not in harmony on many occasions and this seemed to be one of those times, but I convinced my body to go through the trauma of shivering and freezing. However, my body tried to stop me cold at the bathroom door once and a few more times before stepping under the shower. At last, my body gave up, I was convinced of all the worthy troubles and I came as fair as this Snow possessing the other half of the River View Side bench.

Should I go and sit on the top, it must be freezing cold on Poori Mountain. It is just 20 feet high to climb on stairs so there would hardly be any difference of temperature. At least I can take a walk to keep me warm and look at the beautiful scenery. Ah, I am missing a cup of hot tea. As it happened to be, I had only had one cup after breakfast while watching the 10 most important national news of the day. National news was significantly different on different news channels. Same nation, different national news.

The host greeted viewers on a positive note of welcoming the cold morning and ended the same statement with the negative notion of the unending cold weather. The Top 10 news sentiments were very religious, as it used to be 30 years ago, only with trickier words and flashier dashboards. Questions in viewers' minds are placed with almost no right information about the topic. Mostly, it feels like they are placing an idea in the minds of the viewer that was not there before to think about. At last, the anchor says, "Think about it until we come back with more bullsh*t".

Although, most of the channels had the same catchy point, among the news of the day was that of the statue maker, a serial killer kind of thing. I was bewildered with the details of it. I wondered how the media could give the killer exactly what he wanted, attention. They had created a cartoon character with a knife in his hand in dark background and crows were flying in the moon's light when the killer was approaching a person sitting on a bench and the cheap commentary of the anchor over it.

Nevertheless, on the same hand media was making people aware of what was going on and how to be on the preventive side. I just hope for the presentation to be different, more ethical or sensible with a kiss of sensitivity. Detailed coverage of the news aired after an hour. The whole thing gave me more chills than taking the bath. I got back in time from grocery shopping to watch the coverage. Though while walking back, I was stressed thinking of all the lives that had been seized by this so-called statue maker and how many more he would take before he is caught hold of. I was amazed to realize that I took so much interest in this matter. I paced my legs to reach the television. There were experts talking about the psychopathic nature of the man committing the crime, his intentions. Moreover, they tried to deduce the motive of the crimes. However, the whole discussion took a funny turn when two of the experts tried to prove their own theory on the killer and ended up in fiery debate with each other.

One said that the killer was taking revenge against the entire mis happening in the world, and that he was trying to cleanse it. The other person said that he was someone who was trying to find meaning in all of this. Over all it was productive to watch, as they talked about the precautions one can take that was agreed upon by the whole panel and there was a police officer to explain how to reach out if one witnesses anything unusual.

God could do better, I think sitting on the bench at the top of Poori Mountain. I can see the estuary clearly, but the formation of fog did not impress me. River looks pale not green, blue and transparent. Dense fog covers the vast sea. In addition, light snowfall will be a nice touch to add to the beauty of this place. However, for snowfall we have to wait for the weather reports. I have always hated waiting but I cannot complain as I am before time. We had an agreement to meet at 3 PM at the River View Side. I reached at 2 and its half-past 2 now, there is half an hour to kill but each second passes like a farts' smell.

I started going through the available and feasible options to pass time. Option 1 is to walk down the road to the coffee shop, have coffee and come back. Option 2 is to go to the public rest room, relieve myself and be back which seems to be a 10 minutes' walk. Option 3 is to reach into my pocket, put on my headphones and keep thinking about coffee and rest room. Giving these options a few second of thought, I decided to combine all the 3 keeping in mind to scrap the ice from other half of the bench with a small tin sheet my eyes caught at the corner. I put on the headphones and started walking towards the public rest room. A good warm walk, while listening the ghazal that says,

"Oh, my love, I wait for you with racing heart

My heart that is you, are you racing too, towards me.

You are still so far away from me.

So, what is that beating in your chest?

If it is not my heart, then where is my heart?

Is my heart longing for you or is it in search for me?

What evil thing is this love?

What belonged to me left me and longs for you.

Even my breath hurts me, why cannot you come to relieve me

from these pains.

Why cannot you?"

The Public restroom welcomes me with a nauseating smell. It is drowned in stinking water as if everyone decided to pee on the floor, leaving the urinal attached to the wall as a decoration. I took a deep breath before entering the radioactive zone. To make sure that the water does not splash and make me wet; I take each step carefully as if walking on the ice. Water drops are falling from a single point making a blip sound, though there are many drops strengthening themselves every second to meet the stinky ocean on the floor. I can hear blips at each passing second, irritatingly letting me know how alone I am. Don't all these lonesome sounds tell us that? The creaking sound in the furniture, the sound coming from door hinge, unfamiliar wind in the closed space, I have never heard them in my life when I am not feeling alone. Once I am in position and finish what I have come for, I exhale, thinking that I can manage to get out of the radioactive zone with no more need of oxygen, but I am wrong and have to inhale more shit then I could have with normal breathing. I remember from my childhood memories when my cousin swallowed a one-rupee coin. Everyone encircled him and gave different advice. Make him drink detergent water (Does not that kill you? somehow, I remember that), drill a finger on the tonsil; try to vomit. Except my cousin, everyone else panicked. We should have found a stinking place like this rest room and made him stand in the middle and ask him to take a deep breath. Forget the coin; even breakfast from the day before would have come out from his mouth.

The Tap is generously pouring water for invisible souls. I try to tighten the tap, but it pours more water and I find out someone adjusted it to the position where minimal water is wasted. If people would have known whom to call, we could have asked them to come and repair.

When I come out of the rest room, I hear funny sounds with each step. My journey continues in the direction of warm coffee. When I reach the coffee stall, stall owner greets me with a smile and reassures himself by questioning me if I am coming from the rest room. Embarrassed, I ask if it is the smell. He replies, "No, for that I would need to be very close and most of the people who come after using the rest room, their shoes make weird sounds and if you're wearing flat slippers then God help you." I assure him that God has important things to do and he does not worry about people slipping and getting wet in dirty rest rooms. Nevertheless, he continues over my interruption and says, "There was a time when the rest room used to be clean and tidy, all the flushes worked, and the taps were not leaking." With no choice, I listen about his friend's struggle in maintaining the restroom. He said this as he was still stirring coffee in the pan, so I ask, "What happened." He replies, "Some guy came on a vacation and he complained about him. All my friend did was he charged 2 rupees for peeing and 5 rupees for" and he raises his hand and shows me two fingers. To come back to the topic I said, "Don't you feel it is the right thing to do? It is a public rest room built by the government to use free of cost. Then why doesn't the government maintain it? My friend was charging little money and in return, he kept it clean and well maintained. Sir! The builder and the politician from this area are from an upper caste, and they never come to see what is happening here. All they care about is to put their own and the party's name on it. They do not feel ashamed in doing this." He continues and asks me, "How would you have felt, sir! If you pay 2 rupees for your business for a clean toilet, your shoes would be dry, and you would not smell like pee." I say, "In a time like this, I would most certainly be fine in paying more than 2 rupees." I take the coffee cup and hand him the money. "Thank You Sir!" he says.

When I come back from my expedition, it is 3 PM and time for her presence. I smell like the rest room mixed with the deodorant I used before leaving the house. My mouth is shooting the smell of coffee in the direction I am breathing; this is going to be a smelly date. I look around for her on the benches, below the trees, in every possible direction and the nearby places, but no luck. She must be on the way. It takes courage to come out of the house in this weather and it is hard to get a cab in some areas as well. "I will come", she had said. I had confirmed the time and the place with her, twice. I hope everything is all right. She has my number if something is up and she can contact me. I should have asked her, her number and not just handed over my number on a piece of paper.

Where is she? Why is she not here? What could have gone wrong? These are all the questions that keep popping up, but I cannot answer them standing right where I am. I know all I can do is to wait but the unanswered questions are tormenting me. I do not even know what all complications she has. I am already overwhelmed with uncertain feelings. Moreover, the fact that am getting disturbed thinking what must have gone wrong is deadening my mind. The warmth of your memory has started fading as my judgement of you coming to the place is clouding. The bench is giving me the feelings of sitting on thorns, taken out from a deep freezer. This seems to be the very right moment for opportunistic chilly winds to make their presence felt and make life more miserable. Therefore, to avoid this I start walking briskly around the bench and console my mind with optimistic thoughts. It is not too late to decide that she will not come or something worse. The plan is still in its place, a few minutes late should not make the whole arrangement look awful. As it occurs to me that, she might have come and left not seeing me here, as I was exercising the three options, this destroys my all optimistic thoughts. It is highly possible that she came, sat here for few minutes, not finding me anywhere close, decided to leave. However, that is unlikely as well as I did not go for that long. In any case, I need to be prepared for her arrival and I take the tin sheet from the corner and start to scrape the snow from the bench.

I see a woman standing nearby wearing a long over coat. She could confirm if she saw anyone waiting here in my absence. I approach her and ask if she has seen any woman, hoping to hear no from her. She replies, "I am waiting for my husband". I say that it is all right, but I ask, "Have you seen any woman waiting here."

"No, not since past 20 minutes."

I thank her.

Anyways I sat on the bench thinking:

{If you will not come, I will relate our past to future}

CHAPTER 2

HER

"**O**h boy!"

I can see you; it is very unusual for you to be on time at any occasion as per your old habit and that too half an hour early. I expected you to be at least half an hour late. You were an eleventh-hour person, whether to book a train ticket, a flight ticket, a movie ticket, or anything else that needed a prior booking. And when argued with, you would say, "How about a last-minute adventure?" Well, there were some, and mostly only last-minute running. Although my knees hurt standing here for more than 20 minutes, it is expensive but worth it. The scene is beautiful, the wind is refreshing, and looking at the sea with a dense fog falling on it calms my body that is unbalanced with your thoughts.

My heart is thumping with beats skipping every now and then, just like older and younger times. I cannot comprehend whether I am feeling myself or losing myself like those times when we were bewildered with happiness or we felt scared and happy at the same time. However, this is unlike the moment when you see heavenly beauty, you stammer as you are out of words to appreciate it. I am confused even talking to myself. The fact that I will be meeting you has made me wrestle with the arguments of my rational thoughts. All of this is overwhelming, and I am riding on the crests and troughs of emotions. You have walked in a no-go zone and I could not stop that from happening.

My family was worried about me going to meet someone alone in such a cold weather. I think my daughter read the excitement on my face. She seems to understand a lot these days or I am out of my game. I said, "Meeting an old friend", and all of them giggled and smiled. I felt new, excited and younger; as these feelings that I had forgotten long ago came knocking into my world. However, I manage to show them a pale face, acting in ways, a girl does when falling in love for the first time, and hiding as if it is nothing. Life is perfect, a small loving family. What else can I demand? Only the days seem to be redundant but there is life in it.

You used to visit me in my thoughts sometimes randomly or sometimes at your own will. I could be laying on the bed tired, and your memories would encircle me and crawl inside me one by one. I loved them and never fought them because they were my own. The most unnerving part was that I could not concentrate on anything specific. Even in busy day-to-day activities, you would pop up and I did not have any control. After continuously hearing from people who surrounded me back then -- where is your mind? Why do you look so absent-minded the whole day? I tried hard and took back control of my mind or maybe it was time that did the trick, hard to remember now. Though that did not stop you from completely popping up, so whenever I was alone, we sat for a long time and we talked. I liked it. I used to update you about everything that was happening, from what I did to how I felt. Though you were part of my consciousness that saw all the things that happened with my eyes, felt as I felt but still you sat and listened carefully in my mind at least that was what I believed. Although it was a one-way communication, I used to make sure to call your name and confirm that you were listening.

We never realize as the life goes on -- we are addicted not only to a person whom we are in love with but almost everything associated with them, like calling their names, their ways of responding, how they call our name, how to irritate them, and the list goes on. How much I have missed calling your name. The problem with talking to yourself or thinking about someone you love is that you never call out your beloved's name. But one of the early days, I suddenly realized this, that I missed calling your name. Therefore, I waited and when no one was around, I called out your name, and felt the dryness and emptiness in my vocal cords. When I tried for the first time, I could not say it. Then I adjusted my voice and tried again, it reached by the door and the sound of your name died. How could I let that happen? I wanted to live with your name. Then I called your name out as if you were sitting in the next room. Right then I used to get a feeling that told me if I would call your name loud enough you would hear it. So, this time I tried calling it louder than the last time. After a few times, I always ended up crying like a fool, but I felt lighter each time.

Occasionally you tapped on my shoulder and when I turned around to look to see that you were not there, I thought you must have had a good laugh; I took your shoulder tap as a very bad joke.

A few of the times, you reminded me what we would have done together if presented with situations that happened in my married life. We would be different because you would be there, I used to think and shrug the memory off. I felt tired and wanted to escape from all our memory. Maybe you did not like the idea of being shrugged off or maybe you did not want to see me go through the pain and you finally stopped.

As the days passed by, I tried to live in the present, avoided the past and started to think about how the future would take shape. But there was some power working behind all this that knew when to appear from the subconscious mind and take me back to square one. This happened when you came into my dreams. Life was running smooth, it was almost a month and we had not talked but one night you decided to show up unannounced. I never liked you in my dreams, you were never constant, your face ran around without body, at times fuzzy, and other times so close that I lost you inside me. I had heard from elders that there is a hidden meaning in each dream, but no one mentioned how to search for those meanings, it is just another unanswered question of my life.

With so much to lose at every step of my life, I stopped looking forward to it long ago. I wanted to become a part of my family's life. Be happy in their happiness. I thought this is what was left for me. Then I saw you in the fruit shop. At first, I could not believe my eyes, heart started thumping even trying to recognize you, and at this age, that is a sign of a heart attack. I wanted to run away, at this age that was not an option. I wanted to hide; at this age, I could not sit inside the fruit crates. You saw me and I could not look away, a part of me wanted to, I was not shy but scared. It was as if experiencing death, in a flash of a second, I saw everything happen again, shocked I kept looking at you. I thought you were trying to recognize me, and then you smiled, looked happy and confused. It was always fun to read you.

We were both out of words and our eyes were trying to accept each other with the changes that had happened over time on our faces. We talked for almost an hour standing in between vegetables crates and fruits shelves. Most of the time, we were talking to people, they would say "excuse me" and we would move aside saying sorry and smiled looking at each other. It felt that people wanted to buy specific fruits or vegetables that were only beside us. We ended up asking the same questions many times. "How about your family?" "How many kids?" Hearing about your family, saddened me. Maybe you felt the same about me. It felt nice talking to you after so long, I wanted to ask so many things, and felt like meeting an old friend lost in time but we were not just friends. When the time came to say bye, you asked me to meet you. I wanted to say no, but I could not. I cursed myself later thinking about where my happiness went in the family happiness. I became a different person while talking to you, something came back to life inside me, hope; yeah it must be hope, not so sure as I am not good with words. Let us settle down with hope.

Going back home and almost for the whole night, I pondered a lot about our next meeting. So many thoughts came rushing to me. Am I being selfish? Am I being disrespectful to the memories of my family and husband? What is the point of starting something that has no beginning or end to it? Am I overthinking us? That is how all of this starts. We meet, we talk, and we are stuck in the loop. We start demanding more and more from one another and then there will be consequences. Will I become like one of those women who are part of gossip? They would say, "At such an age, she should be thinking about her daughter but look at her going around shamelessly. She even has grandchildren, what kind of an impression will they have growing up?" I have had enough of this in life, cannot take anymore. Memories came back and not all of them were pleasant. Us moving our separate ways, unbearable pain, and these memories seemed as intact as if it happened yesterday. I will meet him. This will be our first and last. I will make him understand. We are not at the age to think for ourselves. Family, kids, and relations are all that matters.

Seems that you are tired of sitting. Why are you walking towards the mound? It is cold up there. Your walk is slow. You climb the stairs and take two rounds of the tree before sitting on the bench. I burst into laughter thinking you will take seven rounds of the tree. That top must be giving a beautiful view of this area. If we were together, we would have walked hand in hand to the Poori and for our whole lives. Should I go and surprise you from behind, wouldn't that be too much in just the second meeting?

The life that I had imagined for myself watching people around me while growing up and what I got served instead had huge differences. However, I never regretted it for the most part, but there are some. When I was getting married, I could not bear to think how I was going to spend my whole life leaving behind someone I loved deeply. I begged mother to listen to me and to disagree for this marriage. Mother said, "You will adjust with him and once you do, you will be in love with him without even realizing." I was disheartened with my parents and mostly got annoyed listening to all such points to remember in order to have a successful marriage, from mother, aunts, and whoever that was getting chance to speak their peace.

Cousin advised not to have kids for the first three years, "If you do then no enjoyment." Granny, aunt and mother wanted me to have babies in my lap after the first night. All these people wanted me to become like them and I did not want that. They wanted me to carry the same burden that they carried. Even compliments were old. Aunt said, "You look like your mother", granny said, "You look like my sister when she was getting married"; mother kind of understood and just said, "You look beautiful."

I tried my best not to become like the women in my family. Not that there was anything wrong in it, I just wanted to be me. To be truthful, I wanted to find a new path. I had been complimented from my head to toe that I resembled someone else in family. Maybe they said all of this to cheer me up or they wanted me to talk. Most of them even understood that I was building walls to keep them away, but they kept on climbing it as if I had put on a challenge in front of them to try as many times as they wish. All they said was "Do not worry" without knowing my worries. They did not have the slightest of idea about my feelings, but they were all I had. They thought I was feeling what they felt when they were getting married, uncomfortable to share life with a stranger, but I had greater worries.

For starters, I was worried about how to react to my new life partner. I was scared that looking at my face, he would judge that something was wrong with me. After the date of marriage was fixed, my parents' choice tried to talk to me in a seductive tone and I went blank. I felt so wrong as some stranger was forcing me to be comfortable with him and I panicked. I was sure he understood that I did not want this sort of a relationship and that I was not ready. I pondered the whole night how things would unfold, but he said sorry next day, and our conversation proceeded smoothly. If he had seen my face in the panicked state, everything could have gone wrong. He would have asked questions without realizing that he could not hear those answers. I was worried what would happen if he saw my face. I tried a couple of times to wear a fake smile in front of the mirror, but I was not convinced looking at myself and ended up crying twice. How loathsome and sad of a life I had.

I dreamt to create my own life, but the parents had their own dreams for me. At the end, it looked like their dreams were more important to put into action. It was their dream to watch me go to school when I cried not to. It was their dream to see me independent in society, but it was never their dream to let me marry someone whom I loved. I never understood why our generation was so much dependent on our parents to take the most important decisions of life. Is it because we were the first generation to experience a certain freedom of life that the last one did not have? Or is it the emotions? Or is it the fear of taking risk and not working out? Many times, even parents' choices are not right but they will lend emotional support if it goes wrong and say, that it is what god wills.

If we go against our parents, then there is no support and no one will come forward to help, as this is not what god wills. Why does god only will, what the majority wants? Going against the majorities will, you will die alone, no one will be around you. But is it not the case that we all die alone anyways?

There were times when nothing was working, I used to pray to God, but he had his own plan like everybody else. God and I could never get on the same page since then. Now, I just talk to God quit praying long ago. God never speaks back to me, who am I to force if the all knower chooses not to reply. We pray what we want, and God gives us barely for survival and demands our thanks. I thanked him for everything I had in my life, I begged him to make things right for us, and he never did.

Once you were my God, I thought focusing back my eyes on you. I lost the chain of thoughts and could see the same old you. The mind has a nice way of playing games. What deep thoughts are going on in your mind? You must be freezing sitting on the top of Poori.

Now where are you leaving? You need to wait here for me. That is what we agreed upon. Here he goes to God knows where. I cannot wait here for the whole evening. You are only allowed to walk in the direction where I am. Did you think this meeting is not a good idea and plan on leaving me standing here? You have your headphones on; you must be listening to collection of sad songs. I hated those emotional lines; after we were separated, they hit me right on the nerves.

The notion that I will not be able to meet you has started

kicking in and making me feel the same way that I felt while coming to meet you, overwhelming emotion followed by underwhelming emotion, on repeat. I pull myself together and start reasoning. Maybe you went to have a short cigarette break or to have something to eat. Maybe there are hundreds of Maybes that can happen, but I want you to be back at the same place. If you are not back in 15 minutes, I will leave. I will be gone. This is the only chance for us to meet for the first time and the last time. What are you thinking leaving the place just before the time for I reached there? You are not the kind of person I knew I suppose. It has been long, people change. How could I have not thought this before and come running on your calling? I will be gone and will never be back. I start to think of the old days and cannot resist enjoying them. Those days were good. After a while, I see a physique of similar stature as you appear in my sight. I am so happy seeing you come back. I feel the warmth of a hug.

CHAPTER 3

HIS

After scrapping the snow, the whole bench is fit to be occupied. I cannot wait for a change in the weather for the ice to melt, that would be very long process. She can come anytime but she has not yet. It seems as same as the way she never came back to fill the void created by her absence in my life. I inherited the void left by her and that was the only thing that was left inside me after she was gone. I cared and kept on going back to the void and fuelled it with good memories that I had of her, us. The emptiness that kicks in when someone that you love leaves, is like a disease that one inherits from their parents without any choice. It just wakes up inside you.

When I saw her for the first time, I did not feel a remote connection with her. There was no love at first sight, neither on second nor on third. We passed each other for couple of days without any clue of future togetherness. Finally, when we were looking into each other's eyes, neither did I get the feeling to swim in the ocean of her eyes nor to lay my face beneath her hair, that were soft like the wind beneath a tree, nothing. When we exchanged words, it was a quarrel. Then the quarrel went quiet, and we just talked about random things in life. Our random specific questions were to confirm our belief in each other, questions that tested our eligibility to let us in each other's life. I used to come up with questions and your answers completed them. We discussed things about which we needed to highlight our views and then listened to each other carefully to fall in love. We tried hard to find things common between us. I used protective words and you showed protective behaviour. Then I thought of the similarities we had and there were tons of them. Did we start caring for each other because of these affinities? I think it is right to say that we love the likeness of minds first and then the person. All the above created a point of convergence between us that pulled the both of us together, closer.

You talked about how things were with you at home, work and in life. You sounded rebellious mostly. I liked the tune. You described how much you hated taking the approval for almost everything that you have to do in life being a girl. I explained that it was not as if we boys could do anything without permission but agreed on the part of having the upper hand for getting the permission. How much you had to explain yourself to people around you? You seemed tired of it but did not give up. You talked about your cousins and their parents. Moreover, how they influenced your upbringing. How much should parents listen or not listen to people around them while taking decision for their children? Why do we need to take ownership of what we want to do in life?

Everything you said made sense under the moonlight lamp. I changed every night and each morning after listening to you. I was able to see things clearly with your words. Though I felt you were hesitant in sharing secrets. I wanted to know all your secrets, desperately. Things that you had never shared with anyone. I wanted to be the person who could understand every breath and every mood of yours. I was too desperate to know you, but the natural process of love was slow and like any other story, we took our time to know each other and then we slowly slipped into the other's life knowingly and unknowingly. Then you were there in everything I did, and I ended up doing all the things with you, I never thought to do. I even started liking things that I hated in most of the girls. Nevertheless, when you did those things it was lovely. How romantic of me.

I remember your friends smiling at us when we talked, as if everybody else knew the traps we had laid out for each other. We were ignorant of what was happening, that was how the heart shutdown the brain. My first encounter of love was of waiting to eat together and possibly doing all the things that we could do together. Since my childhood days, our family ate together whenever we could. But a strange person waiting to eat with you and who won't eat if you do not, seems very special. Mother's lesson was to be independent and to work proactively. After meeting you it changed from 'I have to do it' to 'we have to do it', my life became full of work.

We were never decisive to be a part of each other; it just happened that we became so close to one another because we had luxury to spent time together. You saw my flaws and accepted it; I saw your flaws and smiled. Again, how romantic of me.

It is so very unlike of you to be late, time has changed you.

Ye zindagi, ye taqlife aur tum

Sab paas kyun nahi aa jate ho

We were happy, at least we had that, and whatever we had was ours. Our decision to come close was an internal influence rather than external one. And all the freedom of choosing and believing, gave us the confidence that we needed in life to be our own pioneer. Never thought love can do all of that in a single slap.

I changed without acknowledging the conversion. I changed for better, people around me acknowledged that, but I did not do at the time. Everything was happening with precision, in perfection that was what I felt, or it was an effect of love. Well, one thing that was certain to me was that I loved you. What could be possibly be wrong with that? Nothing!

Well, there was only one thing wrong with it, "Time". It was time that allowed us to be together. Therefore, it becomes very important tool in ones' hand; be happy until the time we can be together. Once time stops allowing us to do that, we will have no other choice. Well, again what could possibly be wrong with that? Everything!

When we shared emotions with each other, it was intimate, as we do not do that often or with anyone for that matter. We do not share it even with family. Most of us were scared to like someone openly thinking that they will have the upper hand. Most of us were scared to fall in love, so we conned ourselves in doing that. Afterwards, we blamed it on loneliness, career growth, career fall, happiness, sadness, destiny, morality… in short GOD.

When you left, I thought a lot about what caused me to be with you. I did not have any answers. I tried hard, when I failed, I started making up answers. I was alone and needed something to hold on. I had a good enough reason to lie to myself.

If I open all the right doors of memory, and see it from third person's view, we need love to live and we chose each other, may be that was the reason.

Time with you passed as if god had fast-forwarded it and now that am waiting here, he has slowed it down. I think I can put all the blame on all doer, he would not mind.

The idea hit my mind that I should have brought a book to read when my eyes met a boy with a book, sitting with his sister and parents. The whole family is dressed in a way as if they were going to participate in Winter Olympics right away. Childhood days were awesome; one wears flashy clothes, bright white shoes and run in a single direction unless tired. I ran a lot in school, after school and before school, but the fun in running after school was the best. When I was in lower grade classes, a group of children waited for their elder brother and sister as senior classes took an hour more to learn, so I waited too. I used to think that they were slow in learning and everybody get slow once they are old like my grandpa but found out differently. We ran so blindly that every day at least two to three pairs of kids bumped into each other. One day I too bumped into a boy of my class. We never talked to each other before. But we had seen our parents talking, so we had mutual respect. We both got one friend who ran to pick us up. We both laughed getting up. When we both were up, and about to run again.

My friend looked up at the sky and said, "Dear god make it rain heavily."

The other boy's friend did not like this idea and he said, "It should not rain." Else, we will get drenched in water and fall sick.

Before he could complete his sentence, my friend decided to pray again for rain.

"It will rain only if your god has lost his mind", came the reply from the other boy's friend, Mr. Speaker.

"Don't you dare call god mad", said my friend.

I interrupted, "He did not say that."

My friend's two fiery eyes looked at me and asked, "Whose side you are on?" Rest of the conversation I stood quiet, so did my collision partner. The situation was escalated when Mr. Speaker decided to punch in the air and said, "This is for your god."

"At least, our god is sitting on the cloud and we cannot see him because he is far, where is your god?" asked my friend.

Mr. Speaker said, "Our god is everywhere, in the walls, in the trees, in the earth."

My friend looked at me and said that, "They pray to everything." He Jumped high and hit the ground hard. Two hands punched in the air and four legs jumped.

Next day had no surprise, same boring classes, teachers entering the door saying, "Good Morning" and we all stood up to greet her back and exactly forty-five minutes later, the bell went off to signal her that she could leave saying "Thank You!" I hated going to school but the recent event had made it less boring. So, I made sure to attend school every day. Most of the time we four eyed each other and my friend and me waited for other party to make a move. Initially the beating of the Gods happened twice in a day and we hesitated to do it in front of other children but the beating multiplied day by day.

Next thing we knew, the whole class was confused about the punching and jumping. Neither they nor we told anyone about it. It might have gotten the four of us in trouble, mutual respect. One day my friend came to me and said, "We need to be together always." "Why would that be?" I asked. He said, "That they got me alone and punched 16 times. I had to jump alone 8 times. Tomorrow it might happen with you as well. Therefore, from now on we must be together always in school. We go for breakfast together, library together; we will hang out during play period together."

In our second last period, I whispered ---- I need to go. My friend said, "It is fine to go alone they are busy in copying from black board." I went alone, roamed in the toilet for a bit and when I was about to start my business, two figures appeared in the toilet. Looking at the opposition party I said, "I do not want any funny business here". Collision partner's eyes agreed but Mr. Speaker ruled against it. He started punching and so did the collision partner. He confirmed the number as 40 and

divided it by two and said, "You have to jump twenty times and said with an evil laugh."

"No, he will jump 10 times" came the voice of my friend and "10 is on me." They punched we jumped. I was glad to think that I did not have to jump holding pee. Funny thing was they used only one hand to punch and the day they realized this was the last day for punching and jumping.

The English teacher was sitting on the table and was correcting our test papers when my friend hit the floor with both his feet and the sound of boom echoed. In reply, Mr. Speaker head of opposition party punched in the air showing this to fellow students. Collision partner's eyes turned towards me and we both exchanged a glance of embarrassment. Miss Anza our English teacher said, "umm hmmmmm" and broadcasted, "Concentrate on reading. Whoever is disturbing the class if I found out them, five marks will be deducted from his paper", the threat made me comfortable that there will not be any god business that day.

After five minutes, there was boom with a silent punch. Either she was not interested in correcting papers or she got bored after doing it for half an hour, it was hard guess to make but this time she got up and asked, "Who did it?" Everybody was silent in the class; no one said anything, mutual respect. This respect always seems challenging to teachers and it had similar effect on Miss Anza. She asked class monitors to get up and tell her who did it. Two were standing, a girl and a boy, right to equality. Boy kept quiet saying he was reading and did not see who did it. But the girl monitor told the whole story of four of us after Miss Anza threatened to deduct five marks from class monitor's paper, as they are not doing their duty properly. These two jumps and these two punches one after the other. Miss Anza called the four of us to her desk and this confirmed me that she is not interested in correction anymore and I would not know about my marks that day and five marks would be less the next day.

Miss Anza was one of the teachers whom you just know once you have noted her presence anywhere in the school campus. Though she taught, only junior classes but seniors made sure to wish her greetings. None of the students' fathers missed parents'-teacher meet for class taught by Miss Anza. She was fair, milky white fair. Round chubby face, big cute eyes, nose and lips justified their presence on her face. Her back was flat, only her shoulder was visible and looked as if kameez suit was hanging. She covered her chest very gracefully with a dupatta. My young eyes could see only this much but she was very popular. Growing up in a town where everyone knew who was up to what, most of the guests at home asked directly or indirectly about her. She was a treat to be in class, never scolded her class, and that was the argument presented by her students to brand her as the best teacher.

"Who wants to go first", Miss Anza demanded for the third time and declared, "If you people want to keep quiet about it then get your student's diary." My friend started first, thinking he will have upper hand on the story, if he would not have, I would have said it myself. Once Miss Anza twisted my ears so hard that it pained for two days when I tried to wiggle them. She had big nails with red paint, ones that were too flashy. She was a hot favourite for most of the students, but I never liked her. Mr. Speaker spoke next. Collision partner and I kept quiet the whole time. Miss Anza heard intently sitting in a posture of praying in church and said, "It is a sin what you four did. Oh my god, it is even a sin to think about beating any human beings or animals, leave alone hitting. One should not think bad things about god." She looked confused about the topic to me. She added, "You four should be ashamed of yourself. I have never seen such kids who dare to beat god." Then seeing bright shining shame on collision partner's face and mine she said, "I did not expect this from you two." That really hit on nerve of Mr. Speaker. How she could not expect this from me, my left ear felt confused. Miss Anza has played divide and rule policy on four of us. We were not of age to comprehend this; the effect of this policy was that there were two new teams, team one has two bright shining shame faced kids and team two had unstoppable lips.

When Miss Anza realized there is not an ounce of shame on the face of team two, she threatened to call the parents of the four of us. Team one stood firmly but the team two had four crying eyes. My friend begged that his father would beat the shit out of him in well-mannered way and Mr. Speaker said that he would run away from home. That shook Miss Anza.

Miss Anza took the polite route and explained to the four of us that if we beat the gods, he would not love us. We four should apologize to each other and to each other's gods. "Why do we have different gods", asked collision partner. Miss Anza replied, "Both gods are same." Then said, "No all gods are one god." I thought this woman was confused. Miss Anza commanded us in polite manner to do as asked and we did. She was successful in scaring us from god, more than an evil monster.

The next day while having breakfast other party proposed truce and so did we. I was feeling relived that I can go to toilet alone without thinking about punching and jumping. One of them said, "After getting so much beating, Gods must have cried but we did not hear him." My friend confirmed with the highest authority that it rains when god cries. I said, "God does not cry, instead when a person does something wrong, god makes him cry." I confirmed to them that it is true because mother said so. They all agreed, as it did not come from father. Would God make us cry asked Mr. Speaker? "No if you apologize, he leaves that person alone, God is very forgiving in nature" mother said so.

"Why does he care only for the wrong deeds and leaves alone good people?" one of them asked.

"No, my mother said he calls good people to him when this world becomes a bad place for them and keeps them in heaven, so, it is not a good idea to be good."

Both teams punched and jumped.

The Winter Olympics team left, I am alone with unending thoughts that is drifting in my entire life.

Har saans har pahar ghutan si hoti hai

Mere ilm mein hai ki tum bhi raaton mein kam soti ho

Tum jab saath thi to sab accha lagta tha

Aisi bhi kya thi ki aisa lagta hai

CHAPTER 4

HER

I never expected to see you and look at you this closely, still so far but I know what I mean. Nevertheless, that is life, and it gives birth to unexpected situations. After coming so far this is what we learn that life goes on no matter what happens. All your memories were archived after we decided to move separate ways. However, I drank from them whenever anything reminded me of you.

Usually the deep voice of anyone around me triggered your event in me. This was how weak my body used to get. My very first memory of you is your voice that made my head turn. I could not see you, only heard you. I was sitting on the first row and you were in the last. When you spoke, your voice tickled my ear with soft blows as if it touched me and I turned. I was irritated about losing control. Who was that? I could not see you, but your voice was recorded. Next, when I heard you in the cafeteria, you were standing next to me, same voice, boosted and I got excited to see the owner. The fact of liking a stranger and getting excited about it, I never comprehended. It seemed dangerous, like playing with fire consciously and unconsciously. I wanted you to be in my vicinity, somewhere near me, neither too close nor too far.

My heart felt heavy when you were not around; waited eagerly, eyes and ears were on the lookout. Once you had satisfied either of these senses, I felt relaxed. I was happy with what I had from a stranger, did not expect more. I could not trust a stranger based on his voice or the features that I had fallen for. Such things happen often in one's life but that does not certify anyone trustworthy or good enough to hang out. I am no expert in matter of affairs. One of my friends back in college days had a thing for library boy. He was cute but then he was a library boy. I was like, how could you? She said, "I am not going to marry him, I find him cute. Did you not read in school that there is no bias on caste, creed, race, religion, age, sex? When we fall in love, we need to take all into account, so, let me at least stare at the library boy." Once I had possessed this information, I was on a constant watch over her behaviour. She never missed catching his glance whenever he passed in the canteen, delivered sets of books in class, walking on the ground, in the auditorium, or at any place where she could. Her face would light up, eyes flared, and her lips gave way to her light yellowish teeth's or she did all of that to tease me. She made sure to return all of the books issued by him to him and she waited for him to return the books in his hand if he was not there.

Most of the time, I was like, "What is wrong with you. Is this not getting a bit too much?"

"This is all the fun I can have, let me be happy" was the reply.

Monitoring my friend's behaviour closely, I got so involved that without realizing I started behaving like her, partly. Partly was that I never missed checking out our library boy. Yes, he was cute, curly lustrous hair, pointed nose, visible jaw line and this was when I reminded myself, he was a library boy. Later when we had one of our closed room talks, we found out that most of the girls checked him out and that the library boy was married and had a one-year-old daughter. I was relieved to find out that this was common and there was no need for my conscience to be hurt. This was the point where I learnt from my friends to enjoy what you like in darkness. Do not let people know your liking, especially that particular person whom you like.

Not that I wanted to be alone, I wanted to be with someone trustworthy, someone who will not take advantage of my vulnerability, someone whom I can give my boxes of secrets to guide. A couple of times I dreamed of myself failing in my love life. Each of these dreams made my heart drift away from love. Dreams that made me aware of the pain that I will endure if a person, whom I cared for deeply, cheated. These dreams came as a lesson to me not to fall prey for animals. Once I was awake, I made sure not to fall for any traps and decided if there is any risk involved then there is no me.

These boxes of secrets were very special for me they contained all I had. I had protected them and kept them in locked rooms. Behaving freely, lovingly, emotionally, caringly, and all the things that I had never shared with anyone, as I felt scared to do so. I could not do hit and trial with guys to find out who will care or who was that one person. Few of the things in the box will be new even to me; I was not sure about my own reaction and got scared to go back and look for some of the boxes myself. Few boxes I checked and closed them so tightly that even if I felt that I wanted to open them, it required a considerable amount of strength. These closed tight boxes would help me not to slip in front of the guys with ulterior motives. Other boxes had things that I found I was capable to do with someone new, I left those as it were, a new experience, though I thought about it but made sure not to utter a word and let anyone find out. I protected them and was not ready to take a risk with anyone.

Once I found someone trustworthy, I wanted to roam freely and let the special person protect me, even though I would be vulnerable in his hands. I needed to make sure that the person was serious about all the boxes full of secrets. Some even had my anxieties or most of them were pack with it, hard to decide. Later I changed my mind and decided to open boxes one by one, monitoring how he behaved just as I monitored my friend checking out the library boy.

All my planning failed when we talked. I tried playing safe, did not want to blow it, didn't want you to understand that I have a liking for you, naturally went on my defensive behaviour and ended up being rude. Not a much-appreciated move though, it came to me as natural human defence. I thought about my friend, how she would have reacted while talking to library boy and all I could imagine was her smiling face. However, when the situation cooled off, you confessed as well that you wanted revenge for my rudeness and made sure to make my preferences in daily life a bit hard. The more you gave me hard time, the more you thought about me. This is how your brain tricked, in order to give me hard time; you have to go through the hard time with me.

I suppose there are stages of falling in love. Once I was playing safe and even rude to you, then I was having constant thoughts about seeing you. My emotions were not under my control. I looked forward to meet you anytime, anywhere but I could not ask and I kept quiet. May be this desperation also came out from one of the boxes? Never ever in my life, had I felt in such a way? I was back again in a scared state. Wanted things to fall in place for us. I wanted you to be with me badly. In desperation, I told my friends about you, for guidance or ideas, they said that I was going nuts and it was not a good proposal to move forward. I concurred with them, hid my emotions right after showing them. I hoped that they would understand and support me, but they did not. They thought it would be right for me to be just friends with you. It was too late. I failed to take their advice and felt happy about that later.

Someone heard me, when I said that things should fall in place for us and then the beautiful nights came. The most special time was when we talked in the group and everybody used to share their story and leave once it was late, post-midnight. You never left early, and I did not want to leave you. I waited for the moment for us to be left alone in our whole day's routine, so I could hear you in isolation from all the noises. No one to disturb us. How perfectly was I able to relate with all your stories. Even the ones that were beyond my understanding. You talked about your last relationship. Moreover, the time that you wanted to spend as the mourning period for her, with packs and packs of cigarettes annoyed me the most. You talked about your dreams of doing something big, investing in business, building huge homes to accommodate everybody you love and care. Protect everyone around you. All your anxieties were in your dreams, I could see. I wanted us to talk until the fireball came up, birds started chirping, horn honking, people waking up, but I could not say that. On the same hand, the special good night with your two lines of *sher* unbalanced my mind to accommodate our separation until morning.

"Aakhen raaton mein sone he kahun deti huin,

Teri yaadon se muh dho deti hain,

Subah ko es baat ki kaafi shikayat rahti hai,

Ye raatein to saari yaadein loot leti hain"

You might be thinking about your lost love, but I was building a memory, that would in future wash my face whole night. Everything was going as unplanned and I was happy about it. There was no reason to feel otherwise, until your friends started screaming your name when I passed. I felt it was an attack on my secret life, though I never reacted. Deep down I was scared to think if this would ruin what we had, I got repulsive of the fact of you being with them. Although it occurred to me in my mind that your friends meant to have fun, this was my first encounter with unknown special feelings rushing inside me, and I wanted it to be very special memory in my life. I wanted to tell you not to listen to anyone, not to talk to anyone about us, but it was all in my head. I too wanted to scream like your friends, I could not; I was scared that someone will hear, or no one will care. All the worries went sideways when I found you standing by my side quietly, cutely!

Days passed and with each passing hour together, we grew addicted to each other. At first I was very cautious and then one morning or evening or noon, I don't remember, didn't know what I was supposed to do, I gave up my guard and placed my head from your shoulder to right where I could listen to your heart beating and realized that your heart skipped beats just like mine.

I see you getting weary with waiting; I do not feel I am ready to walk to you yet. I am juggling our memories of being young in love, stupid and careless. My body is recharging with all the old times' memories and seems capable enough to process. I want to talk to you.

CHAPTER 5

HIS

I look around for your presence again; my eyes meet a couple staring back at me. They are walking while holding hands in a weird way. Not exactly holding hands, their fingers were curling around each other, all of them. I tried doing the same with my left hand curling the right-hand fingers. It was painful and after a few seconds, the bones started hurting. It is an intrinsic nature of love, pain. Stupidity tops it.

The fact is, love comes naturally with its pace like healing, both cannot happen in an instant. Falling for someone's beauty makes us go crazy about them, which could be as simple as their long hanging hair like a horsetail or them ignorant of their own beauty. When we went out as friends, we talked, went around to see places with others, but nothing went to my head to kick-start my heart pumping for you. The very first thing that led me your way was your hand, and I am still confused about that. Your hands were the most beautiful hands I had ever seen. Fair and the light green veins started from the bottom of the fingers like a thunder lightning and vanished at random spots in your arms, this thought made me laugh every time.

I look back at the couple and they were not interested in me anymore. Now, I doubt they were interested even at the first sight. This time I am not able to isolate their body part and they were so entwined in each other. Back in my days, couples were more conscious about people around them. Who might see them together, who may put a word to someone who knows a person who knows their family or relatives? There could be hundreds of troubles and adventures when meeting someone. There was more than adventure if caught. Once my friend during my college days went for a night out from her girls' hostel, using some genuine excuses she made to the administration. She went on a bike trip with a couple of other friends. They drove long before reaching some hilly area that they had booked for night camp. There was campfire and they sat, danced and had good time around it. There were other students, family groups around them. She said that it was a very good place to hang out and had an awesome time. The twist came later when her father in a Facebook post saw her hanging between two boys. A friend of her father tagged him in the post, shared by one of his family friends; he wanted to make him aware that the next time he visits his daughter, he could go see the surrounding places as well. Rest was cruel history. So many stories I am reliving today that are funny and hilarious now, but not then.

We hid each other well and we were never caught. A part that I regret and cherish at different time. We were a couple but friends, we were together but separated, entwined but isolated, our love hidden from the world as we were. At least we believed in our belief. Thinking about togetherness, entwining and the belief system of good old days, makes me even more uneasy to wait here. The detailing and the third eye perspective of my own life is giving me too much enlightenment to handle.

I remember how the ignored fact popped up like a haemorrhoid, very unpleasant to sit on and had the capacity to bleed if left untreated. We wanted to neither sit on it nor let it bleed. We acknowledged the trap and wished to resolve it. All we were able to do was reason with ourselves and with each other. We did what any one would have done, panicked. We wanted to run away from everyone, each other. There was strangeness in both of our nature for some time. There was no help and it was highly important to kill the matter. Therefore, we forced ourselves into relaxed state. It was relief but just for a moment.

Nothing changed except the relief moment, irritation came back to us and we panicked again. Repeated circle from in relief state to irritation, thrice. After exhaustion of the vicious circle, we realized it was going to happen eventually, it is our forecasting right from the first stage, our prophecy. We were the false prophets with the right prophecy. Situation was one of a kind, I was scared to pull a wrong move, and you were scared to lose everything. I managed to show my cool and proposed you to leave the matter for some time until it knocked again.

I saw you disturbed, again and could not resist a second to ask what was wrong. At first, you hesitated to tell me what was going on between the two of them. I insisted further, when I came to know about the calls in detail.

"This will be over once your mother is tired and do not worry yourself further, it was her job as a mother", I said. I myself was unconvinced by my answer.

"Mother is very adamant this time", you said and came back to you strongly on all the criticisms of the marriage.

"I am dragging the topic since last one year, I do not think I can do it anymore", she added.

"This time it is intense. This kind of call is happening thrice a week and the level of heat was increasing as the number of calls increased day by day."

Listening to all this, I took a deep breath and could not think of any resolution at the time and kept quiet.

Nevertheless, it was the need of the time and for the sake of peacefulness in our small life, to have an estimate of our trouble. We had to know what monster we had woken up. The thesis is since we had absorbed our dedicated time together, our whole world can collapse in void at any moment. We were unknown of this place, void. Our new home together but separated. We were free to shout, and it was guaranteed that neither one could hear each other, nor anyone could hear from outside. We were free to roam around in nothingness with no time limit. It was a perfect place to be. We were again scared to our teeth and desperate to know the cause and we deduced agreeably and instantly that it was "time" which seemed to be the main culprit here. And thus, to conclude the expert analogy of the matter for which there was no help, we ourselves became the experts of the present situation, after failed prophets and thus concluded that it's the avoidance factors' partner shipped with time which perpetrated it to cause so much trouble. We were convinced and contained to comprehend of how our reasoning over the matter had shaped up. Hence, I was calm and she too concurred with me.

However, it was not very long that your mother discussed again a new marriage proposal. Once your mother caught on that you were ill responsive to any questions, she took the matter to next level abruptly. And made you recount all she had suffered as a woman for her upbringing. How much she had fought on behalf of you, to send you to school and then to study far away from home. Things were never as it looked like; she made it easy for you. It was just the starting of never-ending rattling unless agreed to the matter. Your mother also pointed out, who it was that convinced everyone at home to give permission for you to get a job in such a big company. Who was always there for you, no matter what? Moreover, the calls used to end trying to make you understand that how important it was for you to establish an exemplary example by listening to them, on the choice of the groom followed by, when to marry to the time to marry and say yes to marriage. Also, stressing on the fact that you are the first girl to reach this height and will be the reason to open or close the door for other girls in the family. You took a deep breath and hung your head low.

We kept quiet for few minutes and looking at you, I said, "Can you please discuss the matter in agreeable way with your mother?"

There is no reason to quarrel without telling her about us. Nevertheless, I understood that your mother might have a hint of what was coming and was building her defence strongly. Your mother did all of this in a much-planned manner with a kiss of maturity, a necessary technique we learned in next few decades as parents.

"It is time to hit back", you said after a couple of days. Well, not in any scenario, I can do that, I said and laughed. "Do what?" you enquired. I said, "Hit your mother." You did not talk to me for 2 days. When you did, I had apologized for 48 times. You did not let me complete the half century. I could have boasted about it later to you. The idea to act so soon was not convincing to me, and I advised you to wait more. It is already getting very late, you pressed.

You were putting continuous efforts from your side. You urged that it is too early for you to marry. "It is never too early or too late; we need to find a right partner for you," said your mother. "Moreover, this person might be the right one for you. We have a good feeling about him."

"How could you think I can marry a person just because of your good feeling about him?" you said.

"This time it is not just me alone, your father is supporting this proposal as well. In addition, you can talk to him yourself and meet him. No one is asking you to say yes blindly. We want well for you and you have to consider this." Your mother was putting every excuse of your at the side.

A lot happened as time passed, we fought over every new person's proposal that your mother made. Went out for dinner, then planned a Goa trip, went to Goa, from Goa to Pondicherry and from Pondicherry back to Goa, we had good time and were unstoppable. Therefore, I settled comfortably in my world with the hope that nothing will happen, and we will live like this forever, happily.

All the difficulties will eventually pass was my belief and time will do its job until you got commanded by your parents to meet a person in person. We were devastated; I thought our world was crumbling down. The week before the week to meet this person in person, you got a call from your mother that she does not need to anymore. I was happy but enquired why, what happened? You said, "Not sure, mother did not tell me why." I enquired yet again feeling that something is in shadow. That is when you lost your shit and gave me thunderbolts, which forced me to think that my whole life has passed. I'm still unable to figure out the situation when a woman wills a man to ask more from her and when to keep quiet.

I felt the irritation was crossing the threshold limit and it was time to hit back. With the same fire, I conveyed to you, let us do this. You looked happy and relaxed. The bigger question was whom to target first. You proposed, "Let me first talk to my father, once he understands, mother will not be an issue." I agreed saying you understand your people better.

It bugged me daily, how you would start the conversation, how your father would react, how you might be reacting in your head. Thousands of questions were forcing their presence in my head. Until one day when you said, "I did talk to my father." I stared at you in an unbelievable state that you did. Happily, which was not the case of your face, but to make you feel you did a very proud job, I demanded the full script of the conversation. I asked you to sit down politely and requested to start from the beginning. You started by saying, "First we talked about this and that." I stopped you instantly and asked you to begin again from the point when you said hello on the phone. You begin again calmly with every detail. However, we both were eager to get at the point. "He is a very nice person, cares for me, supports me, and corrects me just like you. Once I was sick, he got medicines for me at mid night." I smiled and said, "And?"

"And, this and that. Can we get to the point now?"

"Fine!" I said.

"My father said it is impossible, he couldn't believe that I even brought this to him." I knew very well where everything will go south, still asked you to take a step back and tell me when and why father said that.

You exhaled tons of carbon di oxide and said, "Everything went well until I was telling about you. Then my father asked, 'Where he is from?' and I said 'Pluto', he himself guessed that you are a Muslim."

"Why did you say Pluto? It is not even a planet you could have said Mars. People are dying to go to Mars; they even want to establish a colony there. Why cannot Muslims have something good like Mars?"

With a pause of silence, you smiled, and I smiled back and said, "All we can do is try until there is no way our parents agree." Your father asked to keep this conversation between him and her; he was worried for his wife to get sick knowing about the situation, you agreed. You took my hand in yours and said, "I am very hungry." We laughed.

The topic was revisited, and father assured her that if and only if the guy is from same religion and of any other caste, even the way below ones in hierarchy, he could have considered. This proposal is way beyond the limit of agreeing to consider it. Let alone try it. This time I was also listening to the call with one earplug. Your father explained to you the gravity of situation, which he believed you did not understand. He said, "Our religions are like two riverbanks that can never meet." I muted the phone and said, "I will build a bridge and we will meet at the centre point." You smiled and said after unmuting, "Please father he is not like that, he understands me better than I understand about myself."

Your father replied, "Even your mother and I had not spoken to each other before marriage. We believed in our parents and look now we have lived our life so peacefully and are proud to have each other in our lives." He spoke nonstop for more than 3 minutes, which in short meant this could not happen in any universe where she is his daughter and we are two different riverbanks. This time I said, "I am very hungry" after the marathon call was over.

After two days, your mother called and gave the news that your father was not keeping well. She had a feeling that something was consuming him, may be some tension related to work and enquired from you of knowing anything about it or him sharing anything to her. We knew the reason when she told me about this call. For the sake of being on same page, I asked you to tell our tale to mother. Call was scheduled on a weekday, as we did not want our weekend to be the worst weekend in the history. She initiated the topic by saying, "There is this guy and I love him."

"What is wrong with you? Why are you so much straight forward with your mother when it came to tell her about us", I muted and asked? She said just, "Wait and watch; her reaction will not change if I tell this in a long and happy story." Your mother bypassed your straightforwardness each time and I understood one thing that student is challenging her master.

"Okay, now tell me where he is from, who is he, and what caste?"

"Well he is Martian."

Now there were three people not feeling so well, you, your father and your boyfriend.

As soon as her mother learnt about me, she started cursing, and said that she knew that something was going on. "How she could let this profanity affect us?" and disconnected the call. We both looked at each other; neither of us were hungry that day. However, I took both of us for ice-cream treat after getting the whole idea why you wanted to talk to your father first.

Couple of days passed and there was no call from her parents' side. Therefore, I asked you to call back after few days and enquire about their health; you resented the call but were eager to know about them. It took you some courage and time to call your mother and the call started with the inquiry, "Is he there with you right now?"

You lied, "No, he is not, which gave some relief." Rest of the call went well with inquiry of well-being of each other.

We did not plan enough; we did not know what we would be doing after rejection. I wanted things to go back to the time as they were before speaking to her parents it simply could not. Your mother made very sure of it. I thought she took hit on her pride and could not accept that their home be tremored because of some outsider. She cursed me on every call and gave her a kiss of emotional blackmail by saying, "If anything happens to you, we both will die or if you try to elope, you would be dead to us." In both options, someone is dying. This made us very uncomfortable and affected our daily life badly. I saw you fighting, crying, putting up defence for me in front of your mother, every time on the call but it was in vain. All of this was affecting both of us, more you than me. I noticed irritation in you throughout the day. Your smile went for the long drive. Your forehead tensed and eyes were restless. I wanted to make all of it stop.

Therefore, I thought it was time to remind you of our promise. Promise was not to fight and keep our cool, how much ever the problems were, even while going our separate ways. Though I was frustrated, irritated with the thought of you leaving. I needed to make you understand how to behave like an adult and try to make most of our time together, but the promise itself did not care about anything except to be kept by the promisers. There was no substitute of our addiction in each other's life, no manual for coping up. Neither promise cared for the memory of all the things we did together nor what we could not do. I wanted to punch it, go berserk, tell how many changes it needed but it was too late. It felt promise was hollow, yet it was hard to keep. It took birth with our love; it was part of trust, part of us. It reminds purity of our love. Promise was childish but it grew to become a woman in me and man in you.

After combating and then convincing myself the worth of our promise, I reminded you about it. You enquired about the reason for reminder. Trying to dodge the real reason for a few minutes, I said, "I am worried about your style of handling our business with your parents. Decision of your parents has affected both of us, I am trying to live with it, and it does not seem to be the case with you. Not eating on time, sleeping less, being absent minded most of the time even when you're with me and all the worry on your face are the culprits for reminding you of our promise. In addition, we both are aware of the extension of the promise, which is no matter what you will never leave your parents for the sake of our happiness and it was more than clear to us from the very beginning that for the marriage like ours, no one is going to give blessings. Religion is a big monster, it has consumed billions of lives in past over the course of time. We are not even the food stuck between teeth. All I am trying to say is to not be so hard on yourself. It is killing our time, which we could have spent in more lovable manner."

You listened to me very intently and said, "I am trying to make us happen. I want to do this, and I will not let my attempt hamper our time anymore" with a smile at last on your face.

We pretended to be very busy in our work. I was thinking of

my life without you, it was a new scenario and I had lot of things to think about it, followed by tears and swollen eye. My problems in life has always over shadowed the beautiful things I had at the time. Rest of the things gave me anxiety. You overshadowed everything, for so long that I became a believer in a happy life. You were in everything as you meant to be. I had the best time of my life. All the little things I had done with you gave me good memories and made me very sad after you were physically absent. The list goes on, from eating sweets in a shop to standing in an ATM queue. How could we hate all those lovely times that we had spent with each other, just because a few people disagreed upon it? The situation became very hard on both of us. What to do? Stop talking, meeting, and curling up like fingers with each other? We never thought about how to limit ourselves from each other's lives.

When it was time for you to leave, I did not show you how angry I was. Something switched in my mind and I wanted to see you cry. Never in my life, would I have wanted that. I had feelings of revenge; wish to do something that would break you down. I wanted to say things to hurt you, but I did not. I wanted to ask you:

Will you kiss him back if he kisses you? Will your hand slips on his shoulder and your head bumps into his chest; will he be to you what I was to you? Will you miss me the way you are not supposed to? Will you feel guilty when my memory knocks off your present life? Will you just let me vaporize from your mind? Will you …

When you were gone, I had you in my mind so very beautiful and facing the reality could distort it. I used to think how my world has changed since you left and how it will be restored if you came back. "Come back" consumed my whole time. What could happen for you to be with me? Some kind of disaster that involves a tragic incident? Why does it have to be like that? Why cannot it happen in normal circumstances?

Was I becoming like you, the way you used to think and say? You left a part in me that demanded you. You left a child back, he cried and lamented for you. I tried hard to console the baby in me, but he never listened to me. I wanted to make sense out of what happened with me, us and I thought very hard....

Difference lies in the greatness of time, once you were there standing firmly with me and then you had to go but I was not ready to vacate the place. I stood there firmly without you. How could I leave the place, it belonged to you, us. I named the place after you. Head, heart, eyes, and lungs – all the organs that participated in loving you kept quiet and experienced the tragedy with no reaction at first. When I called upon them to put blame on and avail justice, they did not speak as the child was quiet, still, not realizing that he would not be loved anymore. The child in me thought you will be back and so did all of the organs. When they did not get the love, they acted like an addict. Eyes kept on shedding tears to swell themselves. Heart palpitated, lungs fought for breath and head chained with your thoughts. My first guess was the head that forced me to think about you, but it did not do that always, most of the time it was busy in calculation of worldly problems. Then I thought it was the eyes that were addicted to see you, daily I saw your picture to satisfy my eyes, it still did not work. Lungs were out of option as they worked with the heart. I was sure that I caught the culprit, but it was not as easy as I thought. They were all together, working in sync and deceiving me. All of it became clear when the child in me took over the mourning. I called for the debate and an open challenge. Head, heart and lungs were on time, but eyes were busy in washing the memory like a warrior fighting for his nation. Each drop had some memory of her, heart and head were enjoying the cleansing, the child could not let it happen as if eyes were trying to steal toys. This child was always there to remember you. When someone showed their love to dear ones. Eyes would tease passing this information to head and heart, waking up the child inside me. My eyes did not want to shed more tears, but the child was in control. I was stuck in a vicious circle.

Now you are back, and I am very happy. We might live all the moments that we dreamed. I would not say that I mourned our separation for the whole life. In Islam when the husband dies, the woman practice Iddah for her husband for 4 months and 10 days. She should wear simple clothes, should not apply kohl to her eyes and use no perfume. I stretched it a bit though, as a man mourning for a woman, does that makes me un-Islamic. While going through all of this, I treasured all the memories I had of you and recreated them in my mind more joyful than when it happened. I ended up being a happy sad man.

Iddah guzaari thi humne
Tere firaaq mein,*
Wasl ke ehsaas mein

*firaaq - separation, wasl - meeting

CHAPTER 6

HER

In love it is mostly like linear regression, it shoots up and continues to do so, but you can calculate the status of the relationship for short interval only, not for long. The time we spent was a part of the shooting up towards the sky, afterwards gravity played its role, and it was a zigzag line until we made it to the ground. Nothing special about it, if I put it like that.

We were in a big city, the most glamorous as people said with the zeal of excitement and happiness, from the possibility of twinkling like a star to be an idol of the people. Everyone was looking forward in making his or her place in people's heart. At the same time, every single one of them complained about the traffic, the busy life, and having no time for themselves and family. We too were part of this huge place, part of the traffic, the busy life, the schedules and part of complaints. We were yet to find out what/who we were. The journey had just started for me, with you; I was looking forward to all the things.

In our time I felt very special by taking a walk, going for ice-cream, smiling at you, watching super-hero movies and you waking me up, listening to you talk non-sense, shopping with you, eating with you, being seen with you, playing with you, debating with you, and the list goes on. One thing that stood out and I felt uncomfortable and thrilling is buying cheap tickets of the front row seats and changing it for executive ones, once the movie starts. Every time someone entered, you would say, "This group have booked the seats we are sitting on. You whispered in my ears even when we were living our separate lives. As if you knew, you just said that to scare me. Things like these I cherish in our memory always. Not dining in expensive hotels, watching movies in gold class. Rather spending time with little or no resource, which made it very special. These were good memories but not something that you would post on a social networking site.

Everything that happened between from not being serious to being serious was very fast, like a beggar's feeling of getting hundred-rupee note that happens in an instant but he craves for it all the time. In no time, we were begging for our happiness from our parents, this society, and last but not the least God.

The chain of events spurred by my inquiry of what is the meaning of love jihad. We friends were sitting when someone initiated the topic that made me ask you about it, later. You took a deep breath, looked at me intently and said, "Yea, something flashed on media channels now a days." You stammered, looked away, paused a lot while explaining and there was heaviness in your voice.

You said:

Jihad means strive to struggle within oneself against sin and meaning of love we both know. There are other meanings of Jihad as well; one is war against enemies of Islam. It is a versatile word and depending upon people's intentions, they can take different meanings from it. The word jihad is not like a word "God" that points only in one direction. Love Jihad means, "A Muslim man luring a Hindu woman with love for the sake of converting them to Islam." However, there is no official evidence of such things happening.

"By combining Love plus jihad, does not it means struggling in affairs of love", I asked.

"It does not work like that; people understand how they want to."

"That was some scholarly level talk", I said smiling but your face was still serious.

"Do you have any other questions?" you asked.

I laughed and said, "No that is all. I just wanted to know what

Love Jihad is."

You stared at me and said that this is no joke; people are losing their lives over it. A Couple is blamed; the guy is still in jail and the girl in house custody. The girl even took police help and claimed that her own people would have killed her if she had not asked for administrative help in time. Even the cops are not of great help, and they cannot save you from everyone including your family. On top of it, there are fringe groups involved in it and all their beating, threatening and killing is conducted by the brainwashed and paid mobs, so, this way no one is to blame.

By the time you reached explaining about the couple who suffers your voice was polite. They made sure that the couple never met each other and harassed, taunted the girl to lose hope to see the guy.

"Religion is not the only player here; it is ego to show off who can take shots, who is more powerful. Ill people surround us even in the twenty first century, but I would like you to read reports and decide about the topic for yourselves. Never listen and believe on things, you need to read, understand and learn to take the right side."

"I am on right side", I said placing the side of my head on his shoulder. You took a deep breath and said, "It is fine to go against the world, I do not care but going against everyone you know ever is the hard part."

The topic was over not its intensity in the environment. Muscles on your face were not loosening even when we met the next time; you were withholding ease of talking and behaving. I liked the way you were acting for some time, serious, dominating, one-liner type of person until then I did not do my homework of reading. Therefore, I decided to go through the articles later in the day, by the time I could recall to read we wished each other Good Night. I thought it was never too late and typed Love Jihad on Google. There were post from Indian media houses but then I found articles from foreign media houses that were respected globally, even abroad people knew about this, but I did not.

"At least download the apps. You will get notifications about things happening in the surrounding", your voice echoed in my head. I started reading articles from Indian media houses and went on to read the foreign ones. Each detail mentioned was heart wrenching, there was no hope in any of the article for the couple to survive. Most disheartening was to read how their family treated them, the father of the girl complained to the police that her daughter was raped, molested and harassed by the guy. He got all the support from the fringe group looking out to communalize things. Society stood with him when they were reminded that your daughter could be next. Everybody treated them awfully. No one cared about asking the right questions, no one cared about what the girl wanted, no one cared about anything that really mattered, each participant had their own agenda to accomplish. Every account of what was happening was regretful, pathetic and disturbing. Somebody even posted names of all the girls dating Muslims guys on social media and called upon the people associated with their group to take revenge from the guys. How did they come up with such a list? Who are these people, why cannot they concentrate on their life matters? Fringe groups have requested their fellow men to lure Muslim girls as part of their revenge strategy; these people have outsmarted the cheapness of the devil.

Most saddening part is that there was no one the couples could turn for help. The Police seems to be of little to no help, a guy was beaten mercilessly by the fringe group members and they kept hitting his private parts over meeting a girl. While when the same girl was escorted to the police station by cops in the car, a female cop slapped her continuously with lewd remarks, recorded by another cop sitting in front seat of the car. I could not help but research what further action was taken against the woman cop over her bitch like behaviour and the other cops who were present and did nothing to stop it from happening and found out they were suspended. I wondered what impact that suspension would have brought on them and their family, only to find out that a politician with substantial power appreciated their actions. So, from an administrative part it felt as if they were there to make sure you went through all the torture alive and be an example for everyone learning.

I ended up reading the materials until 3 AM in the morning and the conclusion of this exercise was that hard times were yet to come. I tried to think of the possibility that my father would go against me and what would I do in that case. Next day when papa called me, I could not talk to him normally as I used to, thinking of how the victim's father treated her. Papa asked me, "Do you have money? Are you well? Is everything good in office? Did you eat? Neither could I tell what was bothering me nor did he know about it to enquire, but later when he did know about it, he did not care to ask.

I understood the reason for his seriousness over the matter after that. He was scared for us because the idea put forth was that if you love someone who the society does not allow you to love, people will punish you severely. People are the judge, the jury and the executioner. At first, I thought it was similar to the idea of god that there was a rulebook and if you went against the rules, you had to be ready for the wrath of God. However, even in the case of God's book, the people were the first to be the judge and the jury. The execution part is sometimes immoderate that is killing and the other times it is moderate that is beating couples to an extent of putting them in the jaws of death. People who carry such burden of being the judge, the jury and the executioner are heroes for others who do the same thing with their filthy mouth. No space for a second chance, apologize to people and you are under their approbation. Apologize to god; he may put you in the heaven. Seems familiar. Who is imitating whom, I wondered? The concept of heaven is either wonderful or sold and marketed beautifully where you live your life freely on your own terms. But people are god in this world, and we are in hell.

"That sounds correct, you are getting smart", you said when I asked him.

I remember your explanation that if we die a good person and get to make it to heaven, we can do anything. Drink liquor, have multiple women and possibly do all the impossible things that are prohibited in this life. Oh yea, I gave him a good tantrum over "multiple women". Then he compensated by saying, "We can do whatever we want to do, and I will want you."

"What will I get? Will I get whatever I want?"

"This is how heavens work", he said after a pause.

"Your answer does not sound confident enough for me."

"Well, I do not know what I will have in the afterlife for sure and I do not know what any women will get in the afterlife. We need to either read about it or ask the right person", he said.

"Let us concentrate on our life where we are living and make it so wonderful that even god's heaven envies."

Next morning was no surprise with all the education of current society, I learned. We were at his place, I was lying down on his bed and he was sitting on the floor, I felt the thudding of windows on the verge of cracking the glasses. He looked at me and smiled with a smile that said that everything was all right, but I had a worrisome feeling deep down in my heart. There was a shadow of a person walking behind the window, from one to two shadows, then three, four and the sound of hundreds of footsteps. A few of them were slowly chanting like a tribesman before offering sacrifice, that grew louder and louder in a few seconds. I wanted to hold the windows to stop them from falling apart, I wanted to protect you and tell you that nothing would happen to you until I was there. You were drawing something, hiding from me. "You will see once it is complete", you told me. Worried alone about all the noises coming from the outside, your head was still down, concentrated on the drawing.

I wished to ask you to let me see what you were drawing and how much you had completed. You would get irritated and say, "Let me finish first, you never listen."

Suddenly, the sound of footsteps and the chanting stopped, and I felt relieved. Whatever it was, it was not near us anymore and passed. You were safe; I waited for you to look up and say, "See what I drew for you."

I saw a half part of the drawing; it looked like a printed picture, perfect. I wondered how you knew to draw like a professional. Maybe you wanted to surprise me when there was a loud thud on the door. I was startled, he looked up and said, "Do not worry I am about to finish, you will be glad to see."

For about a minute, I looked at you and thought about who is at the door, I was scared to death. I tried concentrating on things that were in the room. A scenery was hanging on the wall, there was a small hut in it, isolated from the whole world, the river was flowing at a distance and there was a man carrying wood on his head, he was wearing a jeans and a white-collar shirt, he looked like you. You would bring wood and I would cook for us. Why could not we move inside that picture on the wall? A place that was safe with no restrictions of who can be with whom. How much time will we have to think for other things to do in life?

My eyes met a crack on the wall; I thought if it could be big enough for us to fit, we might find a safe place, a hidden world. The crack was snaking behind the picture hung on the wall. The idea excited me, may be this crack would lead us to that hut in the picture. A twisted journey like the shape of this crack and once this world was a better place we would be back. In the meantime, no one should fill this crack with cement.

My imagination overcame by a loud thud on the door again, I looked towards you, but you kept drawing. I waited for you to say, "It is all right, do not worry." Then there was the second thud, then the third, and then the fourth. It sounded like four hands were banging on the door at different places. In an instant I felt claustrophobic, as if there were hundreds of people standing around the house. The banging on the door shifted to the wall slowly by a random distance. It started from my left side and made a full circle back to the door. Someone is joking with us and having great fun, I thought, running around the house and banging on the door, walls and windows. Must have happened before, being the reason that you are taking it very lightly.

When the circle of thuds completed, and the person was back on the door, he banged on the door twice and then steel rods with loud chants hit the whole house, from all sides. The television on the wall displayed a page of a social media site and written on it was "The whole scene is choreographed.

Groups of people have been paid to participate in this activity and there are some zealots as well. We as a society believe in justice."

I could not understand what they were chanting, and I wanted to shout that there is no one here. But my ribs tightened, and the air was sucked out of the lungs, I started crying with my mouth open and could not make a sound. You stood up and without looking towards me, went out of the room. Once you were out of the room, the noise from each side stopped. I waved my hands to stop you before you walked out of the room. The last sound that I heard was as if someone lifted the door and kept it aside. Not a second had passed and it felt so quiet. I got up and ran towards the door; there was no door, but a lot of people.

I went back into the room to check if everything that was happening was connected to your drawing; you drew us, and you were wearing a white shirt stained with blood. Cracks, paintings, TV, and other showpieces in the room were vanishing one by one or two by two. I came back at the door and shouted, "Where is he?" One of them pointed towards the group of people. Bare foot, I walked outside, and a group of people stood in a circle in the way tribesmen stand after sacrifice. There was no murmur of chants, no noises, no familiar faces, no faces with shame, may be three or four. I desperately wanted to find you, so, I pushed one after another person to get inside the circle. There was a torn apart white shirt stained with mud and blood. I clutched and took hold of it in my hand. I stared back at them and shouted, "You killed him bastards! You killed him!" All of the eyes stared at me coldly as if they knew and waited for me all this time to come right at this place. A few of them left the circle but the ones who stood there looked at each other and acknowledged something that I could not comprehend.

An announcement happened, "Thank you for your participation in the first round. Let us begin the second round. Those of you who are registered for the first round only are requested to leave or stand aside to view the show."

Some left from the circle and other people filled the empty spaces. Slowly they moved their hands and took out the skullcaps from their pockets. I cried, cried and cried to wake up. Throat felt dry but I did not want to drink water, I wanted to stay in this painful state. After so much going on in the mind, finally, when I was able to shut my eyes for a few hours, it resulted in such a horrific dream. This was what god has planned for us.

With such a horrific dream, my day was followed by a mood swing, cursing god, cursing everyone around me, cursing people chanting god's name after sneezing or when they felt tired as if god cared that this specific person in the whole world sneezed and took his name. "What else do I need from humans?" Why do these god loving people not leave us alone? It was the right time for my beautiful mind to present hundreds of possibilities that could happen, and I thought about each one of them in detail.

If I went with my choice, *maa* had prophesized about one death in the family, but she was not sure who that was. By the sound of her tone, I thought I might be included in the list. As I was not sure about your side, I could not think of any death so that made one against zero. I did not like losing, so, just to draw the matter I would count one from yours as well. In addition, my choice might attract unwanted people in our life, and they would be successful in making our life hell, then there was my dream that was horrific.

During lunchtime, you came to me when I was about to scold

the *chai wala* for making the tea extra sweet and you broke the news that you called your mom and told her about us. For some time, it took my mind away from cursing the *chai wala* and everyone.

"I told mother about us, she got very excited, and then she kept quiet."

I recalled how he stopped me and said, "Tell me the whole thing from the beginning as it happened." I demanded the same. You looked at me as if to ask what was wrong with me and started:

As-salam-ulaikum Ammi

Walaikum-as-salam my son!

"Do not try to be over smart and tell me properly I interrupted" ---- you smiled and took out a piece of paper and your cell phone. That piece of paper contained the future and it was:

- General questions
- Caste
- *Khandaan*
- Family values
- Religion

I asked you what these points are. You replied that your conversation started and ended in this order. You said that you did not want to mix it up, so you wrote it down. You had recorded your conversation so that I could hear it myself. Then you could explain if any explanation was needed.

"Now, if I may start", you asked offering me one earpiece of headphone and I nodded.

- General Questions

"I told my mom that there is a girl and I like her. She got very excited by this notion. I could figure out her happiness from her enquiries.

"'Is she from your office?'"

"'Yes, *Maa!* She is from office.' And then she started acting as if she knew something was going on with me ---- showing off her motherly instinct."

"'How tall is she?'"

"'Tall enough *Maa!*'"

"'Where is she from?'"

"'What does her dad do? What does her mother do? How many siblings are they? Is she fashionable or old school? Does she have long hair or short hair?'"

"'Come on *Maa*! I do not have time to measure her hair.'"

"'You need to tell your mother how she looks like.'"

"'Medium length hair cut in steps just below shoulder.' She laughed on this."

"'Is she fair? Not that I care, but how does she look?'"

"'Her complexion is one shade darker than mine, but with some touch up she shines.' I laughed and she did too."

"I am two shades fairer than you are, you liar. Now continue", I said with a smile that you wanted me to have.

"Then we talked about this and that", you said pausing the recorder.

"She asked how much you weigh and all sorts of general questions. That's it."

"Please do not do this and play it", I requested.

- Caste

"'Okay, since you have liked a girl in another city then she must not be *Sayed*.'

"'That is correct *Maa!*'"

"'Beta you know how it is seen in the society that we are living in. People believe us to be the direct descendants of the Prophet's family. Even when you came home after finishing college, I remember you asking around about the *Shijra* (The family tree book). How could you end up liking a girl who is not even *Sayed?*'"

"'I had curiosity at the time; people use to ask me about it. Moreover, I had doubts that even after 1400 years and almost 200 years of the British Empire ruling in India, with so many people migrating, died and killed, how the people survive to maintain this book. Don't they have anything else to do other than maintaining a book ---- who is marrying whom and who has how many kids?'"

You looked at me and said that you did not want to know about it just to brag and it was a genuine doubt. "Okay fine continue", I said.

- *Khandaan*

"'You know how people will react in our family if you do not marry a girl from *Sayed* family and discontinue such an old family tradition. Every single one of your cousins has married in a *Sayed* family. If the girl is not from a *Sayed* family, she will behave differently, and she will do things differently. From eating to sitting and standing, other people's ways are different, and even you used to make fun of it.'"

"'*Maa!* This is not fair to her if she cannot copy how you, aunty or grand *maa* did things. I would certainly not want my wife to copy you guys, let her be herself. When the aunt asked you, what kind of a girl you are looking for, you said that you wanted a girl with different thought process than our family, and I used to make fun of it, as I was not that old.'"

"'Yea in just two years, you got so old that you understand everything now. You know how much I liked your Aunt's daughter, your cousin *choti* but you were not ready.'"

"Who is this *choti*?" I asked, "And why am I hearing about her only now?"

"I can explain all of this in detail later", you requested.

- Family Values

"'How will she understand our family values? She is coming from a different background, she has seen things happening differently, and all of this will be very hard on her. Can she do it? We do not want to lose you from our family.'"

"'*Maa!* Do not try to deviate the topic. Moreover, marrying a girl of my choice does not mean you will lose me.'"

"'Yea, I know you are sensible', *maa* said."

I smiled on that point.

"'It is something that I have to convince the people in the family.'"

"'*Maa!* But'"

"'No beta this becomes serious. You know how the people react in our *khandaan* for marrying outsiders.'"

"'No one is marrying outsiders *maa*.'"

"'I understand, and I do not have any issues with it. I will look for the right time and discuss about it, referring to how the time has changed and all that. I am positive that they will understand.'"

"'Thank You *maa!* I knew you would take a stand for me.'"

"'How could I not for my raja beta?'"

- Religion

"'*Maa* but there is one more thing' and I hesitated. She told me 'Don't you worry and tell me everything.'"

"'She is not Muslim.' This is the point from where she kept quiet; and replied only in 'yes', 'no' and 'hmmm.' I could not tell her how badly I am in love with you."

You looked into my eyes sadly and said, "If only you were Muslim" and I replied, "If only you were Hindu."

We both knew our parents would have done drama even then, but both of our families were mature enough to not go on a killing spree for caste, but religion was still a big thing. After hearing your side, I was in a better position to conclude that even on your side people would react in same or worse manner than mine; we were so similar when it came to do unlawful and painful things.

I was not able to decide what hurt more, were it the plans that I had thought to implement after becoming one with you or was it the time that we had spent with each other or was it the place that I had given you in my life. Even I was full of genuine unanswered questions but there was no book for help. The hardest part was the reaction of my parents; I had thought worse things would have happened but did not expect the level of indifference they showed towards my life. *Maa* never left a single opportunity to say," Because of you, your dad is falling sick. We did so much for you. We could have enjoyed our life but for the sake of your happiness, we sacrificed."

Days passed by and each day offered new thoughts of separation. What could we be possibly doing when we are not together? We would both be living in the same city but could not meet and talk. How painful would that be? As everything ends, it was time for us to end as well. I was told about the deteriorating health of my father, as per the calls from my mother, where she also said that he kept his hand on his chest while lying on the bed and that I will be the one responsible if anything happens to him. At the same time, their hunt for my life partner had increased.

Finally, one-day father opened up to me and said, "I know that may be as a father I have not lived up to your expectations, but I have tried my level best to treat you as my princess. You went to work in such a big city that I was not in favour of, but I did not stop you. You met a guy and fell in love with him. All your father is asking of you is to leave things behind and return to us being the same daughter you once were."

I returned to them the next year but could not leave things behind, as it was not just things to forget, it was my part, my life, my choice and I was not able to keep my promise to dad. All of the above that happened took a toll on my mental health. From the toughest decision to come to a point where it became so transparent for me to take a call. I wanted to fight for our happiness but found out that there was none if family did not agree. We were emotionally entangled with our parents that killed the courage to take steps that went against them. You were inseparable from thought and parents seemed to be remotely worried about that. I wanted to forget you, badly and desperately. I had watched a couple of TV series about supernatural beings like vampires. When "things" (in my parent's language) do not work between humans and vampires, vampires hypnotize and compel the person to forget. A part of it that worried me was how the vampires themselves forgot about the humans they loved so passionately. I wanted to learn the trick of forgetting someone even having their memories. Maybe it was easier to stop remembering about the person who had no memories of your existence. If these bloodsuckers were real, I would have found one and asked them to compel me to see you in future, as a stranger but life was not simple like a TV series.

Father asked me, "Why are you not smiling? It is your marriage."

I wanted to cry holding him and shout, "Don't you know?" I could not do either of them, rather I looked at him. His beards were losing colour, dark circles were darker than usual and falling on cheeks, wrinkles were winning the battle, I smiled with teary eyes. I thought about you looking at my father, if this was our marriage, your disbelieving face popped up like an error.

I asked you a couple of times, "Why cannot your and my family come together and surprise us? We were teasing both of you. We are happy in your happiness." You looked at me and made the worst possible face you could.

"First you have these fairy tale thoughts and then you tell me about it to know my reaction. This is the face you will get", he said.

"Okay these thoughts make me happy", irritatingly I replied.

"In that case, keep having them", he said wearing smile.

My day used to start with your thoughts. I would meet you today, another good day. Then it went on to procrastinate that my father would call and surprise me, "We both are happy with your choice", right then your contorted face popped up, 'Error: Not found happiness.' The afternoon mostly went by with me thinking who would die first if I went with my choice. And by the evening, I realized that there was only one possibility to save the people that I loved. This were how most of my days went well; the worst ones I still do not have the courage to knock.

Neither you nor I decided to move our separate ways because of ill people creating fuss in society. Rather it was our parents who made us emotionally handicapped to take a decision in their favour whether it was a career choice or a life partner. My deep thoughts shattered when screeching sound of loud speaker reached my ears broadcasting to go home as the order is not to be outside after dark.

CHAPTER 7

HIS

I am all set, enthusiastically ready. I have prepared a flask full of black coffee; even have a few milk sachets in my food bag. If I get bored sipping black, I will mix the milk powder and it will be very smart to have two options rather than one, my dad always taught me so.

Oh, I miss him. He was a nice guy with high moral values and low earnings. He used to wake me up daily in the morning before having breakfast, even on Sundays. He would say family is all about eating together and living together. Mother would smile on hearing she never got tired. When I was young, it was enjoyable. All this small talk and waking up for breakfast, then I started noticing loopholes in eating together and living together. He used to wake me up not to eat together as there was less food and he made sure to finish off my bowl as well if I left anything. He would give me lectures over not wasting food and he would say it is a bad habit and then he would clean my bowl. Mum was getting thinner day-by-day. One day I asked why we could not have more cereals for breakfast and why mum ate so less. He stared at mum distantly and I replied to him with more dreaded look. He saw my eyes, there was rage in it and he was taken aback. He was smart; he put himself together, explained to me the reasons for his failures, and added his high moral values in each sentence. He thought I would not understand the meaning behind his words, his intentions. He was fooling us for years.

After that day, breakfast was not same anymore. I was eating his high moral values daily with my bowl of cereals, slowly and gradually. I could see the build-up and tension on his face. His failures consumed him, and I helped him doing that. He must have been thankful to me before succumbing to death, though he never showed.

All this helped my mum as well; she thought he was her world, but I proved her wrong. After my father passed away, I used to wake her up for breakfast and divide cereals equally between both of us. The need to divide in three was not there anymore and I made sure she finished her meal. I told her she was like an old woman who thinks that she cannot walk without a cane, but she was strong enough to walk on her own. She looked at me in awe and cried. She must be proud but neither of my parents were good in showing their thankfulness to me. However, she could not live a healthy life for long and died. I always felt and believed that charity begins at home and helped my parents overcome their problems. They were a perfect couple. Hope someday I will liberate a couple.

Oh, I should not be grilling about my own past. Today, I will liberate a stranger. Someone who is living in pain, unknown of her destiny. Oh yeah, she is a woman. I chose her at the River View Side. Moreover, it would be right to say that she qualified. She made the list. I went to the River View Side last week, when I first saw her. She seemed nothing at first. I thought she was waiting for someone, but she was not. She stood there in cold for two hours. Maniac woman. Next day she did the same. I felt angry and followed her. I wanted to slit her throat a couple of times in front of all the people, so that they understood it is not safe for a woman to roam alone. I never allowed my mum to go out of the house after dad passed away.

She met a woman on her way back and they hugged. The new woman was consoling her and that was when I understood the bigger picture. She has lost someone very close to her heart and that explains her past behaviour at River View Side. Who could that be other than her husband? She is suffering through the same pain my mum did. I decided to help her and show the world that there is someone out there, who cares. I know her routine of coming at River View Side since the past one week. I expect her at or around 4 PM and today is the day she stops going through hell. People will remember this favour; media will be showing it for a whole week or month. They will say a woman who lost her husband recently was murdered, but there is a hidden message as well. The hidden message would be that the woman was alone. People will get this message slowly; I do not expect them to understand it right away. Not everyone is intelligent in today's world.

I opened the kitchen drawer, and there were a range of biscuits, sweet, salty, and a bit of both. Each pack of biscuits is 10 in number and I am not biased with the sweet, salty or bit of both. I eat three packs at a time, one from each flavour. I would love to have some biscuits with milk coffee, not while sipping black. Never liked the combination. Black coffee has its own taste; with one sip, it takes you to places where you had good coffee. That is pure magic! In this regard, I think blood as well possesses some kind of magic and I will admit that am no vampire. Nevertheless, I did not like the taste at all. I am not saying blood has magic in medical terms, I'm no doctor or someone who possesses such kind of knowledge. It has an unpleasant taste and with each drop in the mouth, the taste and effect ran from the tongue to the head. You feel something new.

The very first encounter of blood on my tongue happened back in the day when I was liberating this woman. I found her when I was having a trouble with my urges. She kept crying and with every drop of tear, she was begging me to liberate her. I told her to her face, "I'm in no hurry and you will receive your justice from my end." She was wearing bangles; you know Indian woman, and their love to have loads of bangles. Well, I certainly do understand any kind of love but not the kind where you overdo it. She was wearing bangles like an extra sleeve, from elbow to wrist. I have to get down on my knees and take out the bangles one at a time. No funny business, mannerisms are an important trait in my work.

On the ninth one, I lost my patience and got a bit harsh while pulling them out. She got a deep cut in her wrist and a small jet stream of blood came rushing out on my face, just as a pee jet comes with little pressure at the end. My mouth was not wide open, I am no Dracula, but a part of that jet touched my lips too and it happened to be the reflex of my tongue to come out and wipe the blood from my lips. I took a minute to understand the taste and ran the mixture of my spit and her blood couple of times in my mouth, up, down, right and left. Nerves that connect from the taste buds in the mouth to brains seemed to have a new experience, just like sipping coffee in the morning. I thought this through, and I am no fool. Two things came to my mind, number one: Is it the effect of my drugs in her blood, which is causing all the effects and the funny taste? And number two: Will I experience it with my own blood? It was no place and time to decide on such things. Therefore, I finished my work with her and came back, I took a spoon full of my own blood, and ran it in my mouth and I could say yes blood is magic. I took three packs of biscuits and kept it in my food bag.

I do not want to miss anything; it ruins my mood and the effect of my mood affects my performance. Perhaps that was what happened with the Delhi girl. She was sitting all alone in the park at 9 PM. I passed by her four times and she had deep black mehndi all over her hand with a couple of bangles and wore thick *sindoor*. A newly wedded girl, sitting in the park in the dark, for what reason? What else that could be? She is not happy with her life. Her husband was not treating her well, like how my dad treated mum. I was able to channelize her pain and it felt like my mum was going through all of it again. How could I let something so cruel happen again? For over a month, I carried my food bag and a sharp blade to the same place, but she did not come. I was restless and thought her husband must have locked her in a room. I knew her house, but I could not risk getting caught and failing to liberate her. For her I would have waited as much as required, she reminded me of my mum. It was a 9-hour shift in the park from evening until mid-night. With only coffee and biscuits, I felt hungry, so I ordered pizza a couple of times. There was also a *nimbu paani waala* right outside the park gate and it felt very refreshing after having a glass or two, but he used to leave early. Mosquitoes made my life very hard and I suffered from malaria for a few days. All those chills in my body, body aches and high fever did not make me lose my concentration from the goal.

Finally, she came to the park after thirty-five days of waiting. I could not believe my eyes at first, since I had a high fever, but I could sense her trouble and felt my mum came to see me, asking for help. I did what was required. After injecting her, I told her she will be all right now and her husband cannot do shit, she will be safe where she is going and there is nothing to worry. She blatantly refused to my face about having any trouble. I reminded her that I saw with my own eyes she was being aggressively talked to by her husband last month. She did not agree to any of it and kept crossing me with her words. She said her husband treated her well. This is what my mum felt throughout her life. The whole conversation with her threw my mood off and I had fever too.

Now when I look back to our conversation it makes sense. She said the same set of things that my mum said. The only regret I had with the whole situation was my bad mood and I did not understand her repeating *"madar... madar..."* and then she grew quiet as the injected dose took its effect; otherwise, all hard work was worth it. I did not like the part of media coverage, the police first thought it was extra marital affair or some revenge kind of thing. They failed to find any proof to back it up. Then they said it was thieving, when things got ugly her throat was slit. Only, after post-mortem they thanked me. Idiots!

This whole incident gave me a lot of learning and the main takeaway was not to listen to women apart from their main story, they all are confused like my mum. Second takeaway was that I needed to be more careful towards myself. Malaria! Seriously that too on the job. Third and final takeaway, I am surrounded by fools. It is time to admit that. They took almost 3 weeks to give me credit. I need to leave a signature was the first thought crossing my mind. On further brainstorming, I concluded it would not be the classic thing to do. A passer-by has to come really close in order to understand. I will be waiting for the police to come and then after taking time and clearing their doubts about me, they would confirm. I wish people to know by just looking at the body, from a distance. They should feel it. How about putting a red flag or of any other colour? This felt cheesy and there is no out of the box thinking. I cannot lower my reputation. I paused my thoughts for a couple of days.

It was the weekend and I was giving myself a treat of ice creams with five different flavours and watching Discovery channel. They were showing old monuments and statues. There was this huge statue and the voice on the TV said, "People passing by distance of ten kilometres can see this statue and know about the place." I thought isn't that great? It is wonderful and a beautiful way of knowing about the place. There must be one statue at the entrance of every city and if there are many entrances to a town or city, the statue should be placed at the most important entrance like the front gate of a house.

That night, I dreamed travelling to different cities and at the entrance of each city, there was a huge statue instead of a cheesy board, printed with the name of the city. I saw a huge gate, and it was the India Gate while entering Delhi, I went to Bengaluru and I was welcomed by the tall skyscrapers of the IT industry, in Mumbai I saw the huge gate that was the majestic Gateway of India domineering over the city. I woke up that morning wearing a smile. I had the idea; I would make the people I liberate into statues so others would recognize my work looking at it.

Well, I was no fool. I understood that there was going to be a lot of research work and preparation involved. Where and what to begin with? I browsed on the internet how to make a statue, what are all the things required. I did not get my answers for making a human statue, as this effort was completely new, but anyhow came up with a list. First, I needed to get material to make a statue. Second, who will volunteer to become a statue? This is the tough one. Who is intelligent enough to understand my cause of liberating people? I do not want to kill an innocent person. This point in my list became a bottleneck in my progress.

That evening I went to take a walk around my locality to freshen up my mind. As experts say, a fresh mind can give you great ideas. I saw children playing in the park, and there were many of them. As I went forward, I saw a kid playing with a dog alone. Why isn't he playing with other children? What the fuck is wrong with his parents? Can't they see what I am seeing? Shouldn't they ask their child to play with other children rather than an animal? How will he understand the pain of other children growing up? What is the point of a human being living if he does not connect with other human beings emotionally? I needed to extend my help to people like this. At that moment I decided, who would become my first statue. I drugged one and brought home. I did a small experiment on it, but I failed. I brought another one; it failed as well, another one after that, and that too failed. Almost, three dogs less a week in my locality and it continued for 3 months. When so many dogs had vanished from the street, I observed nobody was missing them. There are many things I could be thanked for; from people being able to sleep peacefully at night without the barking noises, to having less danger of rabies from street dogs. People must have been thinking who is this person? Where is he coming from? Where does he live? But they cannot meet me in person as they never have met messiahs.

Finally, when my experiment was successful, I had already tried different postures on the statues of dogs; sitting, standing, mouth open and closed. Now, I had to carry two bags, one with food items and the other one with all the necessary items to make the body into a statue. I am taking too many responsibilities on my shoulders. I smiled with the thought. My mum would be very proud.

The first human statue I made was in Gaya. It is a small town with very high importance around the world because of Bodh Gaya at its side. I found out about this when I went to see the gigantic statue of Lord Buddha and the guide told me the history about it. I was in awe for almost a week thinking about it and wondered why they did not make a similar huge statue at the entrance to Gaya. I never thought that I would be giving Gaya a gift on my tour. I always have trouble sleeping at night and to pass my time I went to the only place open at night, the railway station. I went to have tea at the station and decided to roam around for a bit. While roaming inside the station from one platform to another, I saw the stationmaster's office and a constable was sitting right outside on a stool, doing his duty as a responsible law man.

Next time, when I saw the same constable, he was beating an old woman on platform nine. Why? Because the old woman was sleeping on the platform. That was not a sufficient reason to beat an old woman. This sight broke my heart. I went to the old woman and asked why she gave cause to get beaten. She looked at me and said, "You seem to belong from a good family." I felt good but demanded an answer to my question. She said, "I invested my whole life in my son so that he could become an officer and live a good life. He got into habit of doing drugs and died. Now, I do not have anyone to look after me." Upon hearing this, I decided that there is not much to talk further and turned away. While going back to platform one, I thought this did not gave her reason to behave in an uncivilized way. Everyone tries to do well in the world but not everyone can succeed. You cannot take this reason to cause trouble for others. My nerves were throbbing and the urges resting in the silhouettes of my mind came back to demand calmness.

Even after coming back and lying down on the bed, I was still unable to sleep and my urges to liberate someone in help were back with such a feeble thought about the old woman. My mother used to say, "You are an owl." An owl does not sleep at night, maybe because of the urges. How good was mother? I cannot imagine her life without me, she could not have survived. People would have taken advantage of her and I would not have been there to protect her. She will be sleeping on platforms like that old woman and men like that constable would have poked and beaten her with a stick. They would have tried to touch my mum at inappropriate places, just like that old woman because no one was coming to protect her. I will protect her. Where is she now? Is she going to come tomorrow to platform nine? With these last few unanswered questions, I slept.

I woke up at nine thinking about platform nine and felt a special connection with the number. There were parathas for breakfast available in the lodge where I was staying. I had two of them with extra butter and a glass of Lassi. I had plans, so after sipping a cup of hot tea, I went to execute them. It took me 15 minutes to reach a place heavily packed with people, Gaya main market area. All sizes of shops were there, and all sizes of these shops had varieties of clothes, bangles, ornaments, dupattas, leggings, kurtas and what not one can imagine. One narrow lane is snaking into another and people were continuously coming out and walking into one another. Not just people but cycles, bikes, auto, rickshaws. If I stopped people coming from one lane, how many of them would be stuck and cry for help, I wondered. I see more women than men; each of these women have a gullible soul. My mum used to hold me in her hand and take me from one shop to another, I would watch all these women asking for more, "Show me that one from top shelves then show me this one from that corner."

They want to buy a dupatta from this shop and a matching kurta from another and even then, cry: *why am I not looking pretty?* It is because you wanted to outsmart people around you and deep down you know that you cannot look pretty. To calm my nerves from these thoughts and keep my mood jolly, I decided to have a glass of *badam* milk, my *lodge wala* told me its best in the Bajaja road, which is 3 minutes' walk from the main market.

While walking towards my glass of *badam* milk, there was smell of Kebabs from hotels mixed with *bakharkhaani's** coming from shops, which felt delicious, but I decided not to have kebab *roti* here, rather I will have my lunch in Jama Masjid road famous for its *bakharkhaani's* with kebabs. I had *badam* milk, grape juice, special juice and again *badam* milk with two different flavours of chips and sat until lunch in the shop. Then decided to walk to Jama Masjid road for my lunch.

I came out of Bajaja road that ended as soon as I took one-step out of the straight road. I found myself on another road with a different name and another market with hundreds of shops. There was a *pan wala* next to a Lassi shop followed by ten or twenty stalls of milk shakes and ice cream. My mood lightened up seeing so many flavours and I planned to taste them next day.

The straight road took me to the brothel area. Women and girls were waving from the balcony and welcoming me to come up to them. At first, I did not understand, then a guy asked me my budget and I said no. I enquired from the same guy about the Jama Masjid road, he replied to me, "Go straight for 500 meters in any direction, you will find a mosque in one direction, a temple in another direction and a movie theatre

*bakharkhaani - A thick flat bread

in this direction pointing on a straight road." But this brothel remains the centre for all the men. Men get more excitement at this place rather than going to any other place.

Impressed by his words I walked in all the directions, choosing the temple side first. When I reached the temple, I found the place to be calm and clean. When I reached mosque, I found the place calm and clean. When I reached theatre, I found the place calm and clean, a show was going on. Every time while coming to brothel, I found the place bright with lights, happy faces, and drunk people.

I ordered one full naan with 5 *seekh kebab** and sat on an old wooden bench accompanied by old rugged table. There is cleanliness in the place, yet it looked dirty. *Lodge wala* told me that these hotels dated back to 1940's or 50's and more than three generations have run it. Is it the archaic nature of place or do the owners keep on buying old furniture I wondered? Cooking stove was built-using mud supported by iron rods inside. A guy sitting next to the counter was pushing meat in *seekh* and passing it to the guy sitting on stove. Kebabs were lying down on top cuddling *seekhs* and there was room for only five *seekh* at a time, which can be chaos in the high traffic of customers. There were patches of black random shapes on the wall, on the floor and on the table. Later, I found the same small black patches on kebabs, naan and on the faces of shop workers. Who are these black patches? Why are they everywhere? Is it some kind of parasite, and what makes this place so special? Why do so many people come here to have the dishes this place offers and then they go and talk about it

*seekh kebab - A form of dish consisting of a mixture of minced meat, garlic and spices thinly wrapped around a skewer and grilled, usually in a tandoor.

to different people at different places? One day, people will come from faraway places to see the statues that I will make; they will say things and hear more things about my work, and I swallowed the last piece with a smile.

After roaming around the area for a couple of hours, viewing a waterless Falgu river and one of the oldest temples in the town, it was time to go to the station and look for the old woman. She must be gone and would come back to sleep at night on one of the platforms. I asked a rickshaw puller to take me to the station. At every 500 meters, there is another market with hundreds of people in a rush to buy things. Rickshaw took a sharp turn and there was no crowd, number of heads decreased exponentially. As I drew near to station, loud noise was making its way to my ears and with a right turn, number of heads increased exponentially, like a magic. People had decided and had a mutual agreement to stand together only on one road leaving the other making it less important, I thought. Pay sixty rupees, rickshaw puller said. After making the payment, I went to have a cup of tea and thought the whole situation through. What will I say to her? How can I help her? How can I protect her, as her son would have if he were alive? With too many unanswered questions, my mind was boggling.

Outside the entrance of station, beggars were sitting in a line leaving an equal space between them for the dogs to pass. However, between the second and the fourth beggar, there was a triple space left as if someone was absent from class. The first one in line was a man with no legs. The second one did not have the left hand and she could not sit straight either.

The third beggar in line had an advantage of an electric pole behind him and was resting on it. He kept falling asleep. When he was not sleeping, he requested money from passers-by. The fourth one seemed all right, he just had rugged clothes on him. Passers-by were dropping money randomly with injustice and the fourth one was collecting more money compared to others as he was sitting last in the line if someone is leaving the station and first in line if someone is entering the station. This is how the world works, but in my world, there is equal space for justice. I imagined them like statues as all four beggars were sitting in different postures. How would people feel when they look at different postures of statues? A statue with no leg, another statue in bent posture with no hand, people might feel that they are unusual looking at them, but it is the reality presented from my world.

Finishing my tea, I went to look around inside station if the old woman was sitting or sleeping on any of the platforms, but it was in vain and came out finding her nowhere. Now there were five beggars with equal space between them, and I found the old woman occupying the triple space left in between the second and the third beggar. I was back at same teashop and took a newspaper to read. After a while, the fourth beggar stood up and left, one with the advantage of a pole beside him. I thought why these beggars were not taking that advantageous spot and later found out that he was back. They each had their own space and the old woman too. I felt all of my thoughts were a mistake and was taking her much more seriously. She had a job, earning money, spending time sitting between her own people. She was not my responsibility. I was at the wrong place, thought too much about her and probably could be in market tasting all different flavours of Lassi.

I ordered a cup of tea. "On the way Sir", the boy shouted and came up with a cup of tea. The boy serving the tea, he was fast and made a fine pair with the other guy who prepared the tea. They made a great team like Batman and Robin. Would I have a partner someday? I will make the statue, and he would look out if anyone was coming. I will ask him to hold the body part straight for the mixture to dry and achieve the right position. I would teach him all the right ways. He will copy me and achieve great heights in this world. My mind came out from these good thoughts and shifted to the constable standing at the corner. I saw one of the beggars handing over money to him and going in the other direction than where his seats was located. Looking at my curiosity, Robin the boy said, "These beggars have to pay him daily for begging. Otherwise, constable Sir will not allow them." I smiled and nodded in a thankful gesture for letting me know. When old woman was handing over her share of gratitude, constable sir exploded on her raising his left hand in the direction to railway station. What could have he said? I wondered. I wanted to know, badly, so went in the direction she was going, passed her and stood. Once she came close, I took out a fifty-rupee note and gave it to her saying, "Were you not sleeping on platform nine yesterday." She said, "Yes, now I have to pay to sleep there and walked away."

I walked as fast as I could towards my lodge; the whole thing was unbearable to me. How could he do such a thing to beggars? There is no heart in this person. He is the opposite of everything what a constable should be doing. How could he ask money from beggars and then bash them for sleeping in open? Where would these poor things go? I walked almost 3 kilometres with unbearable thoughts of constable treating my mother in the same way. It was 8 PM when I entered the lodge and went straight to the room. I would make everything all right I thought. Saying these words, I took out my bag resting under the bed; waiting to be opened since long time with the thoughts, I was possessing in my mind. I took out a smaller bag from inside the bag, went through all the things inside it, and was pleased to find all the necessary items. I kept it ready for such days and quickly went out to have dinner. There is *Chicken Kadai, Paneer Kadai, Saag, Dal Tadka, Ghee Rice* and *Roti* available, said the waiter. I ordered *Saag, Dal Tadka, Ghee Rice and Roti.* Person sitting next to my tables asked for *Chicken Kadai* and *Roti.* How can people murder animals, cook and eat them? Days are not far when they will behave the same way towards human beings. Finishing my dinner, I walked slowly towards my room, it is not good to run or walk fast after eating. With my bag, I left for the station.

Platform 9 was too dark to find an old woman sleeping from platform seven. So, I walked carrying my heavy bag consoling the old woman in my mind: everything will be all right; you will be able to sleep in peace. Her face kept popping up in my head and changed to look like my mother's face. Her hand touches my shoulder, my face and she say, "My son will do it, I know he will." My father on the other hand thinks I cannot, and he smiles as if his face is twitching and changes to look like the constable. I shout as my mum disappears at the constable's appearance; she gets scared of him even in my safe thoughts. There was no one on platform 9. I decided to lurk in shadows of evilness on platform 9. It took three hours for a pair of constables to appear, they were throwing torch light in all possible directions. Why did not he come alone today? However, I waited for the second round of inspection of platform and before 4 AM, I went back to the lodge.

I woke up and executed all of my yesterday's plan, had Lassi in the market and later at night took the same spot at platform 9 waiting for the constable to show up alone. That night old woman came and slept at her spot. I could not see her face from the distance but could feel the peace as if my mum is sleeping. Right around mid-night, the constable woke her up and she said to him, "I do not have money and I paid you all I had." His voice was polite and said, "Get out; it's *Bada Babu** Surprise visit and he will take rounds of all platforms. From tomorrow, there will not be any problem and you can sleep wherever you want." I could hear the stammering in his voice and see fear in his gestures of hands. He was unusually polite. The old woman stood up and left. Constable went in her direction. Who is this *Bada Babu*? Seems like a higher official. The polite conversation from the constable's side made me rc visit my plans. He helped her, as I would have helped my mum. Constable's way of helping was different but there is a demand of justice here on platform 9. Someone must be held responsible.

It was not more than an hour passed when *Bada Babu* showed up with a small torch in his hand that poured dim light. He sat on the cement bench-facing platform 7, kept the torch in his shirt pocket and lit a cigarette. He lit a cigarette in No Smoking zone; he should be the one to stop people from committing such crimes. Torch was still on, so I could see his face clearly in the dark. I injected him; he must have thought it was a mosquito bite. I sat next to him and asked him why he was not doing his job properly. He said things about higher people and lower people, nobody listened, all the blame game. That was no excuse.

*Bada Babu - Senior Official

Then I interrupted him and asked, "What is the meaning of *'madar madar'*? I heard this from the Delhi girl as I liberated her". *Bada Babu* said that she was right and felt unconscious. Anyways, I completed my job and left with his left hand. He had the posture of the second beggar. I left the torch on; focusing at him as designers do in museums, he was my first statue. From platform 1, I turned to see how it looked. The torch light was about to die, people would find him soon.

Morning came up with chaos in the whole town. Police jeeps were running in all the directions, directionless, people had completely different stories. They thought an official died of heart attack. I was sipping my morning tea when the waiter came running for the remote and switched it to news channel. I made him a breaking news; he was on all the channels. News channels were confirming that the world has not seen anything of this kind. How could have they, I thought. They said that the constable on round found the body in morning; however, murder happened at least 4 hours before. "Our reporter will be interviewing the constable on the rounds." To my surprise, it was our constable. He said that around 5 AM it was dark, but he saw flashes of light and a person's structure could be visible for a second. He thought to check and found it to be *Bada Babu*; he said this line with a face that was about to cry. Reporter took the mike away from the constable and confirmed that the killer was still unknown; police said they would do everything in their power to catch him.

Two things struck me, first: why on earth they were not looking at the bigger picture? Second: why did it take so long to find the statue? Well, certainly, I cannot help them to figure out the reason, but I need to improve. It was disheartening to hear the news anymore, as mostly they were speculating one thing or another. While going to the room, there was flickering light around the main counter of lodge. Nah, flickering light would be too much and not an easy thing to carry around. I needed something that was light in weight and could glow in dark. This requirement needed research and brainstorming. Later in the day, I found out on google that there are variety of colours available online that glowed in the dark and radium shaped stars on top of it will look good. If only this came to my mind earlier, *Bada Babu* would have become like the sky glowing bright with stars on him. How lucky would he have been?

All the necessary items were in place and I am ready to leave for River View Side with binoculars hanging around the neck. The place is beautiful, and it is unaffordable to miss any sights, moreover I also found the widow using binoculars. Thinking everything through on such an important day is very critical. However, on such a day, my mind is heavy with the thought of what kind of posture to give to the statue and this being the reason why I like to double check all the items in the list. I have four beggars' postures and few of the improvised postures as well. Which one will suit the widow is the debate? She can be the fourth beggar resting on the pole, which defines her condition mostly. She is alone, tired and wants support in her life which might tell the story of a widow in an appropriate way, but I have seen media and people getting confused in my last few attempts which forced me to improvise. How about the second beggar with the right hand removed instead of the left, that says an important someone is taken away from your life. Without the right hand, life is miserable. People will surely understand this as they did get the point after *Bada Babu* Statue. Initially they were confused with a different set of stories but soon they realized when issues like homelessness, sleeping in the open, starvation, and what not came into light post interviewing the old woman with few more beggars. The whole town was enlightened with *Bada Babu Statue* on platform nine.

It is already past four and I leave my room for River View Side. I take a government bus with two bags, one hanging loose on the right side and the other one with special care on left. Left one has my coffee and food items. Sky is not too dark but dark enough to beat the moonlit skies. Clouds are cuddling each other so tight at the edges that they are curling outwards. The dark clouds, how hollow they are but never allow the light to pass through it. I want to fly through them; lightning guiding my way, but I will not fall when lightning falls on the ground. I will keep on flying and find my way through the black clouds.

Less lightning falls in human vicinity, it mostly falls on barren lands or dense forest as if they are fallen angels who are ashamed of showing themselves. Moreover, if people witness the lightning, the earth absorbs the angel otherwise they can live human life. Today, neither the sun nor moon will witness me; I will be alone in the darkness.

I get down on one stop before the River View Side stop and walked on narrow lanes. There is Poori; that is at least 20 feet high elevated ground round in shape and puffed, with banyan tree popping out from it right in the middle at the River View Side. The view is delicious, and a small bench installed for visitors to capture the beauty in the front. At the backside of banyan tree people drop coins in a small hole in Poori and make a wish. I wonder how many people have dropped coins there and where these coins have gone. Do these coins get absorbed by the earth just as the falling angels are? Front side bench is my spot. I can see everything from the top. Who is alone? Who is with whom? Who is mine? I will be an unknown god looking to help unknown people with unknown problems. The beautiful scenery recorded in my mind did not have a couple sitting on the bench. I have to wait for an hour to see them go away and rushed to capture spot as soon as they left. This is yet another day with beautiful scenery. Clouds are dark black suiciding at the edges of the Sea very far away from sight. Black clouds and frozen White Sea, they have exchanged their colours.

A man is sitting on the bench, he must be cold and alone, bench and man. Well, I settle down and pour some coffee, strong and black. Even the taste makes me warmer. It is time to juggle my eyes through the area and find my girl. There are a few couples here and there, one ice cleaning truck, hot beverage stall and a woman standing in the distant corner. Is that my widow in the corner? Could be some other widow, not mine I confirmed using my binoculars. Took me 5 minutes to scan every curve, corner, bench, couples' spots, widow's favourite spot and gulped the whole cup of coffee to confirm that she is not at River View Side. I was disheartened to find her nowhere. What can I do if people are not punctual? I can help liberate her if only she shows up. Today could be her last day of suffering. I cannot go to houses to clean everybody's mess. I will not let her define my days; maybe she is not even worth it. I guess other people need my help more than she deserves. How about the woman standing alone in the distance? She looks miserable, as if she has cried. At the first glance, I feel something is wrong with her. Who cries at such a beautiful spot? She is in pain. Maybe even more pain than the widow is in. The widow never cried.

Well, she is standing at the very corner of the River View Side, just the right place for us. When we meet, I will tell her how lucky she is. I will tell her the whole story how we both bumped into each other. She will thank me and tell me how weak she felt and hoped someone someday will come and help her out from her miserable situation. It is almost dark, even binoculars will not help me anymore. I need to move closer to her. I don't want her to get scared and move away. Hence, I make my first move that demanded patience and sit on the bench 10 meters away from her. To show how familiar I am with the place, I take out a packet of biscuits and pour some coffee. She gives me glances and acknowledges my presence in her vicinity. Just like a magician uses long sleeves to hide the trick, food items help me to hide serums and injections. People think I am having coffee and biscuits, but like a magician I do my work in shadows. I am ready more than ever and right at the time I decided to make my move, the constable on duty of River View Side flashes his light at us. Before he could come near me, I slip the injection in the bag. Constables and their torches.

The weeping woman is in alert position. She hurriedly gathers herself together and leaves the place. "What ma'am? This is not the time and place to be", says the constable. "If something happens, people will blame the police. What can we do if people are not alert themselves?" She doesn't even stop or even glance at the constable and keeps walking until she was out of sight for the both of us.

"What sir! Do I have to invite you separately?"

"No, Sir! I will finish my cup of coffee and leave", I said.

"Come on sir, if you want to sit then sit near the Poori Mountain, we have installed lights for peoples' safety, why to sit in the dark? Please finish your coffee and sit under the street light, I will wait", the constable said.

"Would you want one cup", I asked. He hesitates. Anyhow, I pour and give it to him. The two of us slurped and he is now comfortable with me.

"Until what time are you guys on duty?", I asked.

"It is my last round sir; I will leave for the station."

Finishing the cup, we greeted goodbyes and walked our separate ways. He towards the station and I towards light. River View Side is almost empty with random installed streetlights, benches and me. Today is the worst day. I desperately wanted to liberate the widow. She is like a black cat, black widow. She crosses me and I am doomed. Frustration and anger reminded me of my father's days. For the first time ever, a woman is capable of reminding me of him. He is smiling on my face. That old dog and this black cat are friends. They must have some relation; she could be my long distant aunt, Aunt Bitch. Before leaving, I will also put a coin and make wishes on Poori for aunt bitch.

My thoughts swing from widow to the sitting man's silhouette, occupying the bench next to the river. He is the same man who I saw. Why did he not leave? He is sitting as if he cannot afford to lose the occupancy of bench, he must be homeless. His world seems to be dependent upon it, cold and alone. Staring in the darkness of frozen sea. Is there something wrong with him? I shrugged at the thought. Today does not seem to be the day of liberation. However, I decided to spend some time in the drawing of darkness and brightness of lights. Even lights have a limit, they can reach to certain extent and then starts darkness, but they always meet at one point or draw a single line together of their limits. Nothing comes in between them. They fight day and night, without getting tired or maybe they are tired. Nobody asked them as no one asks me.

I cared so much for the widow; prepared myself for days and nights to help her. Felt her pain, she turned out to be a bitch. Then I saw the weeping woman and realized there are other people who need me. I have to be wise in selection, learn lessons and extend help towards everyone. Should I ask this man if he is up for a cup of coffee? He is not even moving, as if he is frozen to death. I coughed loudly to receive some kind of acknowledgement from his side and nothing. Few minutes pass sipping the last cup of milk coffee. He stood and walked towards Poori. As he enters the vicinity of light, I look at him, his face looked sad and eyes were down. He was looking older than his age. That is the magic of sad life. What is up with people these days? Everyone is looking dead sad. The weeping woman and then this man. I end up confused myself, whom to liberate? On the other hand, is this way God letting me choose the worthiest of all? First the black widow aka black cat aka Aunt Bitch then the weeping woman and now the sad man. I turned to check on him, he was sitting on my spot, the Poori front bench. He looks as if he has no desire, expectations, and hope in life. If that is visible externally, how broke must he be internally? If he is the one, then I should not be wasting any moment. I looked inside the bag; the Syringe is dripping serum like a hellhound's saliva. I moved swiftly and in no time, there was the liberator behind the banyan tree and the sad man in the front. No flashing light, no constable, no second thoughts, no waiting for aunt bitch, nothing was between us.

To say this is my third mistake today will make me wiser. Sitting next to sad man and hearing his reasons for sitting in cold made my day worse. The last few words by the sad man:

I was waiting for my life; a few decades ago, she had to go. For rest of our life, she visited me as broken memories. Finally, I camouflaged her successfully between other things. Then, we met coincidently. I asked her to meet me here at the River View Side. She said yes. Her every word was promise back in the day, even the ones she did not said out aloud. I could not leave the place in hope of her coming. Maybe she is here or maybe she did come and leave. If she hears about me, she will come running, she should not, it's too late again this time but she will come, she will come, she will come, she will com…

When he stopped, I look at him; his mouth is half open as if something is stuck in his throat. I looked hard at his face and second thoughts were making space in my mind. He wanted to meet the love of his life. She did not show up just like Aunt Bitch. For Twenty-five years, he waited for this day and an unknown god took it. Neither of us were happy, an unknown god and a sad man. We sat at the corners of bench with a satisfied hellhound between us. Alternatively, bitch and dog are smiling, in rhythm, a smile followed by laughter then laughter followed by smile. In between, they asked, "Who is the bitch now?"

In the darkness of frozen sea, everyone came uninvited to haunt me. From the woman in the park to *Bada Babu* flashing torch on me posing differently to the yelping dogs from the streets. I sat with old incomplete love.

CHAPTER 8

HER

Well, well, well, it has been a long day. I stand there watching what all is happening. Killer peekaboos him with the injection. He is paralysed in an instant, he can only speak, and he tells his whole life story, why and for whom he was sitting and waiting. After hearing his story, which Mr. Killer does like to hear from all his victims, he waits for the dose to take its effect in the entire body. Once he feels unconscious, killer takes off his clothes. He slits his wrist deep and cuts deeper as he goes up until the elbow and puts a white plastic cover around his arm tying it to his shoulder. Killer does the same with another arm with a deeper cut, in a hurry.

Any moment could be my moment, I think. His blood is showering out from his arms, bubbles are popping and after a while, it looks like red lava. I can hear blood making all kinds of funny sounds. Next, Killer drops down to his knees facing his victim and puts a big plastic cover around HIS legs making multiple deep cuts in both legs.

He is ready and so am I; it has been a long day. I take a step forward, one, two, and three, as soon as I pull him; he looks at me and then looks back. He rushes towards his body. His hands are trying to grab killer's arm, collar and hair; he is trying to save himself. He is going through the hands, head, and knife repeatedly. Killer being unaware of all of this is busy making his memento. Well I am looking at him, waiting for him to be calm or at least get tired of trying to save his dead body. I know they all know once pulled out of their body that sense of weightlessness, the easiness that they never experienced and the beauty of dying that everyone can have only once. But, no! They always decide to throw a tantrum instead of experiencing it peacefully. I thought this soul would be different, I was wrong.

I am never tired of watching humans' behaviour right after

they die, most of the time it is something new and they are so unpredictable, it makes me wonder crazy things. I remember the 104-year-old woman. Calm and composed, laying on the bed and praying to meet her lord and husband. She had prayed for the last four years to meet the almighty. She was very kind to the nurses who attended to her needs and showered her blessings on to them. She used to say, "May the god give you the most handsome husband in the world." Nurses would blush and their cheeks turn pink every time. She was friendly with the doctors too and most of the staff called her granny, grandma or *daadi maa*. Why is my time not coming, she would repeatedly ask the doctors, nurses and the maids? Couple of times, she was successful in making even the housekeeper cry by her emotional prayers to meet and see her husband in heaven. She would ask them, how is your husband? Treat him well, once your man is gone from your life no one takes care of you, by god I hope you all never see such days. How does it feel to be so lonely in this life? All are selfish in the world; your husband is the only one that loves you dearly. I stood right next to her bed waiting for her time. Her pulse went down, and I thought this is the moment. I changed myself into her husband and stood in front of the bed to surprise her, right then her pulse goes up. Her deep breath signals she is fighting to live more.

At sharp 4 AM, she made a gurgling sound and took her last breath. I pulled her soul and gave a smile. She started jumping on the bed, crying and shouting that she is dead and repeated "why me?" She prayed for two things for last 4 years, one was to be dead and the next one was to see her husband. I dressed my body to look like her husband; it is easier that way to console and calm the dead. She looked at me in utter hate and shouted, "Why did you come?"

I always think humans do not know what they really want, they just pretend to do so, or they are gullible souls. Now this guy was going on about her for the last 24 hours or more. Sat on a bench in the cold for so many hours. I thought that was the way he would die but no. I gave him couple of glimpses of his lover thinking it might be now but no. Finally, his woman went away, I was waiting for him to freeze to death but no. He was still waiting. If he walks towards his place, there are vast possibilities of him meeting one or another kind of accident but no. People like this do not even get heart attack easily. Nevertheless, Thank God, his killer and my saviour showed up. Now that am standing here looking like his lover, he is busy with himself as if he can do something instead of running towards me.

Well, it is time to break the silence and I ask, "How does it feel to see yourself being carved in, blood flowing out of your body, two strange hands touching you and been unable to feel anything, a miracle."

After hearing me, the good news is that he stops throwing his body and the bad news is he is sitting down and maybe sobbing. In between the good and bad news, he looks amazed, bewildered and gives a very long and deep stare to me. It seems that he now understands what has happened and is happening.

Finally, he stands up and walks towards me. Stands beside me in silence for a couple of minutes looking at the making of his statue then turns towards the sea. Like the frozen dead ice, his thoughts seem to be dead too.

"You are looking like her, but you are so young, same as the time when I met her decades back," he said stammering.

"I thought you would not speak, just like a new bride", I said.

He did not blink his eyes on this. "You can see people from past, very young, the fun in being dead", I replied.

So that is what I am, dead and there is fun in this. "Who or what are you", he asked.

"I am your sweetu, do you not remember?" I give a pause, duh nothing. "Okay then, I am Death. I am here to receive you", I said.

"Do I have to see myself being drained or cut into?"

"You mean the statue-making process. Yea! I mean no. I can follow your lead for some time."

"I have questions," he said this as a question.

"What makes you think I have the answers to those?" I ask a counter question.

"They are simple ones. To begin with, why do you look like her?"

"Today is the day you die; let us just say it is a treat for you. Moreover, there is less drama if a known face is there, mostly."

"In addition, are you here just for me in the whole world?" he asks.

"Well, there is not much of a competition and we can multitask."

"Are you?"

"What?"

"I meant to ask, are you multi-tasking now?"

"Yea! Totally."

Our conversation pauses hearing a song. It was Mr. Killer and he is humming a melody. I burst into laughter. It gets awkward.

"How could you laugh on such a cold thing? Should not you be stopping him", he shouted.

"I am not here to stop him; I am here to receive you."

"Hmmmmmmmmmmmmmm", he does.

"Nobody Hmmmmmmmmmmmmms me", I said.

"Whatever you are, you are a woman", he replies.

"I look like one, do I not?"

"Okay, tell me why?"

"Tell you what?"

"Why did you come as her?"

"Well, are you worried that she will die too? So chweeeet!" I gave a pause, no reaction from him (duh again) then said, "Let me remind you everyone is going to die." I came as her because that is my job to make all souls calm as soon as possible, customer experience. She was the one who you were desperate to meet in your last time. Desperation over.

"Wow! So caring", he said.

"Yea, that is the point."

"How about the glimpses?"

Well, as you get near to the time of your death, it is one of the ways to make you humans know that your time is very near. You had four glimpses, excessively much. I gave you the first glimpse, when you switched on your TV. I thought watching about the serial killer will give you a heart attack and that could be your last moment. But no!

"That means, even you did not know how or when my last moment was?"

"Yesssssssssssssss", I said.

There was a moment of silence, and he looked towards his dead body, sitting stiffly on the bench and said, "Could you have tried to change the way I die if you knew when and how?"

"Well, that is above my pay grade. However, I was pulled from the field at one instant long back."

"Why and when?"

"Reason is even unknown to me", it was with some old man.

"Why bring up things, which you yourselves do not know?"

"Why are you curious even now? You are dead. Have fun!" I said.

"What is next?"

Do not be in such a hurry. You have a last wish to make before going to have seven lives of your own choice.

"Wish", he said sarcastically. "What can I have? I cannot ask for life."

Well, except that and much more. You can go anywhere for as long as I get the call to receive the next person and let me be very clear to you it can be anytime. So, rush.

"How would I go?"

"Think of a known place, close your eyes and voila."

"How would I know you want me back?"

"I will call you."

"Okay then, he said and closes his eyes."

He opens his eyes in his apartment room. He scans bed; bed sheets look clean and properly tucked under mattress. A whole month's dosage of medicines is on the table. He smiles thinking what a waste of money and tries to arrange the bottles and his hand goes through them. There are three towels hanging in the room. One is next to the switchboard. It is very dark for human eyes but there are no humans in the room. The room arrangement was very simple with a single bed and a reading table kept next to it.

A sound of meow turns heads. He stares towards the door and walks right through the walls. There is a cat sitting on sofa and two plates on tables with unfinished food. Someone is here for a party. He moves forward to pat the cat, and then stops. The cat's eyes glaze him, and he looks surprised. He pats the cat and stands next to the sofa where he sat and ate breakfast watching news about his killer in the morning. He is looking all the things in the apartment as if he has come to the funeral.

He rushes outside after looking at apartment for the last time. First, he runs for a couple of blocks on the road, and then he starts running through the walls and boundaries. Having fun, Huh! As he reaches the departmental store where they had met for the first time and the last time, he thinks she must have lived nearby. His search resumes. He goes through the walls, one house to another and one bedroom to another. Cats are meowing at him wildly; dogs are barking and chasing him until the walls. He tries finding her in couple's, children's, and babies' room. All are sleeping peacefully including his body on the bench. He becomes an uninvited guest in many homes. No one is either welcoming him or showing him outside. It is an unknown chaos in everyone's world, in his world.

He stops by a lake separating one colony with the other. There is a road about a kilometre connecting both. He gazes the whole road and jumps into the lake. He stands up and first walks on the water like Jesus then runs like himself. He forgot in all this that he is an old man, now he is not. Once he reaches the other side, he runs freely on roads caring no more for vehicles like a child. He reads all the nameplates of the house. He is the worried ghost looking for someone. Someone special!

He continues running mindlessly, searching for his treasure.

Treasure that he could not have had in his life, he wished in his death. His legs are not quitting and one last time he wants to come face to face with her before time ends. Neither he nor I know how much time he has.

Morning is beautiful, a man comes running towards the Poori Mountain, a jogger, climbs five stairs then goes down, climbs 10 stairs then again goes down, he does this with multiples of five stairs. When he reaches on the 20th Stairs and sees that there are only two stairs left, he jumps on both. He walks two steps and does two squats. Next two steps, he cannot complete and looks at the body on the bench. First, he thinks of a homeless person-freezing sitting on the bench. Once he sees the face, he goes down and runs 50 feet away from the Poori. He takes out his phone and calls the police. In no time, there are more than 100 Police officers covering the whole area. Inspector takes the initiative and searches the dead body to know about the person. A paper falls out from the jacket that reads:

Hello Dear Sir,

Please read the below instructions and do exactly, otherwise the dead body will break into pieces.

1. Do not try to move the body for 24 hours. I have experimented with new material that can result the body to break into pieces if body is disturbed.

2. Do not take the jacket off upper part is fragile.

3. Do not stand closely.

Yours Sincerely,
Mr. Killer

When the expert arrives with few more experts who have studied closely all the killings, they all agree to the demands mentioned in the paper as the killer has a reputation of not lying at any instant. Few of the police looks relieved that killer is done with our area. They shake each other's hand and console what we could have done if it is inevitable. 150 square feet of area barred and surrounded by police. No one can get in, but media somehow manages to zoom in lenses and makes report. Hundreds of flashlights in an hour. Everyone wants their piece to report. Every media outfit will play the clip endlessly, from different angles. Face of the dead body is covered with plastic cover post experts took pictures to find his family.

CHAPTER 9

HIS

Hopeless sitting in front of the departmental store and watching people enjoying their lives in such cold weather, I thought if I have to choose between how unlucky I was during my lifetime or in death, I might end up in a long fiery unending debate with myself. Whole life either one thing or another got me by surprise, and it would be wise to say I was never ready for any of it. In my death as well, it was the same design. I was about to leave in another ten or twenty minutes with a broken heart, but out of nowhere, Killer introduced the poison in my body. Post, which I narrated him my whole life story, why, what and when. Not sure, if it was effect of poison, he took me by surprise being the reason, or I was too desperate for someone to know, I told him all at his one question, and did not even hesitate in shyness towards the stranger. However, he showed sympathy after hearing me and expressed negativity towards his actions, he too wished for us to meet and those were the last few words I heard and felt too tired to carry on anymore and slept. Frankly thinking I felt nothing except a pinch on my neck, there was no pain anywhere in the entire body. There was just this feeling of a sharp object between my muscles, that too only twice or thrice.

She pulled me holding my belly button. At first, my soul's stomach came out and I witnessed elasticity of my soul followed by my upper and lower body. I was shocked and thought it was a dream or the effect of some kind of drug, as I could see my stomach coming out of my body. I could not move, my body parts were not listening to me, I wanted to pull myself back into my body, but I could not feel anything, It was not numbness anymore. I was feeling a lightness, a distortion and someone else in command. I wanted to scream but it did not feel right, so, I closed my eyes to stop all this nonsense from happening and to take back the control, but I failed. From a pinch on my neck to coming out of my own body, it all happened very fast, one feeling of fear to another one as if moments were fast-forwarding. When I was standing, I opened my eyes and saw younger her smiling on my face that felt like horror. Never ever in my life I imagined her so unnatural and beautiful. I turned to face the reality and found whole of myself sitting on the bench bleeding in a plastic cover. I felt a great urge to fight and get my life back to the instant when I was waiting for her on the bench, being normal. Normal was back to being alive, back to being alive from death is not normal. I tried to stop a stranger cutting, touching and going through my body as if someone is checking an animal after slaughtering. I did my best it was not enough. I heard a very long sentence, my very first sentence after dying, the summary of that meant is impossible. I sat down and took my time to understand and rewind all the happenings and mis happenings; it was time to face reality, my death, my her. I stood up and walked towards her. She was standing five steps away, though it felt more, as if walking on a large elastic hairband. My first walk was followed by my first sentence.

In barbarism of my death, questions like why kept on echoing in my head. Why like this? Why cannot I dance with my moves for once in my life without any surprises? Why does god have to prove himself an alpha every time? Why cannot he let me alone once? Why does he have to put his plan in work? Why does he have to prove, he is in command? Why does he want to play god every time?

The whole conversation with death was cold like death. Death had HER face that made the whole dying situation harder than it should be. I could not stop looking at her after a while and she could not stop making cheap and lame jokes. She knew more than I knew myself that made me quite uncomfortable. I could not embrace nor hate her; I was not ready and a moment like this no one can run from.

Once she informed about having a wish, the whole situation changed for me, I looked at it as my second chance of meeting her, more like seeing her. I wanted to fill every inch of my heart with her face. Not this plastic beauty standing in front of me. She does not look like this. In a great hurry, I asked few important questions and with subtlety she answered. This is a second chance that I might never have gotten when I was alive. So, I closed my eyes without wasting seconds to start my second journey of meeting her and found myself in my apartment. My apartment where I have lived for years, my room and my bed. There was a time when these rooms had people coming and going, more than one person and then more than two people. I lived my good days here and all the furniture, doors, carpet, Almira and walls bear witness to it. Then we reduced and became two from three and then one from two, roaming in this big fat box all alone. Now, this apartment has no one just like me, with undying memories or all dead memories.

Isn't all of this like a dream, a bad dream? What is that sound? I looked towards the room door and walked through the walls. A cat was sitting on sofa. Can she see me? Throughout my life, I have heard animals can sense dead people; I moved forward to pat her and then stopped. She moved her neck swiftly towards me and leapt her head forward. I patted her. You remember me. She is the only soul I interacted in last 6 months through food and water. She is here to appreciate at last. I stood there silently; I did not have any other option and looked around my apartment.

This house will make people remember me. When they pass in front of my apartment or when people see my statue at River View Side bench they will say, that statue guy used to live here, in this apartment. May be this area will be named after me, statue guy road or statue road. They will say, "He never troubled anyone, he was a good person, always cared for neighbours, gave things to poor." He stayed alone in this big apartment. We thought he would die alone in this house but see how unlucky and miserably he died, not even a roof was on his head. Then people will be tired of good sympathetic story and will start with a new, a damaging story. They will say this house is haunted; no one is willing to buy it in ages. Owner of the house used to leave alone in such a big house, he must be up to fishy things. They will say they have heard from someone that if you try to buy the place you will end up like its owner, Killer will make sure of that. A few passers-by have seen owner's ghost roaming in the lawn, standing at the gate and weirdly smiling. Children always tend to fall in front of the gate; he does not even leave the children alone; there is feeling like something is trying to draw people inside. Once a thief went inside to loot the house, he never came out.

Different people with different versions of the story, still all of them will believe some of it. Kids will bet on touching the gate of the house in evening. People will try to look inside the window and think, last time there was no chair in this room. Their forgetful memory will deceive them and in return, they will haunt me. After a while, there will not be any sweetness left in remembrance of me. Every memory will haunt this house and me forever. Nobody will ever know the real story.

I could not bear these thoughts anymore and I came out and ran in one direction then another. I need consoling, I need to find her, so, I ran carelessly through the privacy of thousands of people, through the walls, on the water but found her nowhere. With disappointment I stood in front of the lake, it will be morning any time. How would she react once she knows about my accident? I wanted to be with her at the time. In hope, I returned towards the departmental store.

CHAPTER 10

HER

I wait for sleep to come and take me to the dreamy unknown beautiful world where life could be merciful. I wait the whole night. One bad thought is topping another one, all my mistakes are flashing like breaking news and demanding why I did not do better. If only I could go back and take two or three decisions differently life could have been happier. This is what we live for, more. More than now what we have. We complain to the past, imagining unrealistic present and try to picture our different selves. Confidence grows as time passes, we could have been better, but it keeps on getting worse.

I look at my husband's passport size picture glued beside my bed under the night lamp. He is in his early thirties wearing a brown suit, head full of hair. Same suit that he wore in many occasions post our marriage. He used to say, "This suit is lucky for me, makes me photogenic." Our daughter has glued him there saying he has not left us, he will always be here, but I knew he was long gone before exhaling his last breath. At his last moment, I sat beside him and cried remembering the old days when he was strong. I wanted to hold his hand, apologize for things that I had done and had never done and requested him to be healthy again. He did not want that. I asked if he wanted water, he kept looking away. I asked, "How are you feeling?" He continued looking away quietly; even I was not sure what he became at the end. He acted stranger than a stranger. He used to be gentle, polite and caring. "What can I do for you ma'am?" he asked me forever. I could see his body lying on the bed, fighting to breathe in. He did not look at me for the last time but rather stared at the ceiling exhaling the last breath with his soul. I will never know what problem he had, maybe he decided to punish me like this. What a cruel way he chose. If only he told me how he was feeling or maybe he did not want to trouble me at his end time.

A couple of times I wanted to remove his picture, it reminded me of failure at his deathbed but thinking about my daughter, I could not do so. She would ask, "Why *maa*?" and I do not have an answer that can be said aloud. With all no's in our marriage, there was still beauty as my mother had forecasted that I would be in love with him without even realizing. I do not remember exactly how long after our marriage or exactly when he became a part of me. He was there each morning and evening. How could you resist falling for someone after spending so much time with them? I started to love him and his existence in my life became very important. Still with all of the love and care, there was a separateness in our lives.

Initially, I used to wait for him to leave for the office; the whole house is for me once he steps out. I used to lie down on the floor in the drawing room and think about my past love. Yea, after a while it started to feel like cheating, guilt as big as a tonsil in my throat. Even after all of this, I felt empty after he was gone and missed him night after night. We stopped talking on the bed late at nights. Neither did he ask why nor did I, we were tired of talking. It just happened but I miss him sleeping next to me, at least someone was there, someone who cared for me. This bed feels larger than this home in the nights.

Both of my eyes are desperate to welcome the darkness, but the monsters are winning. They bring painful memories that rest and wait for the right time to resurface when it hurts most. I had the same feeling the night when my father passed away. I received the news next day that he left us in the mid night; the doctor said that heart attack took him. My brother did not inform me in the night. He wished me to have at least good sleep for that night, but my gut kept on churning and palpitation of the heart said that something wrong has happened.

I was fighting to sleep, and my husband was snoring peacefully with his mouth half open. I never understood how someone could sleep making such growling sounds. Despite that, I was used to it. His snore was a roar of a lion in my deepest and darkest forest at night. Funny things used to come in my head in the dark room with his snore. It felt as if we were attending a marriage ceremony in the dark night with electric generator on. However, many a times, I woke up shivering and his snore was the only thing that confirmed to me that I was safe. I never knew when between his *kharr khurrr tarr turr* I slept.

When I asked him one day in the morning, I could not know when I fell asleep with your generator on, he looked at me and smiled. That day he tried not to, but it was inevitable. I got worried when he did not snore, kept on checking him, missed it for many days after he was gone. What I realized later was that I was not used to the silent nights and the unfriendly nature of sleep made my life more miserable.

Anyways, I did not sleep that whole night. Was it better than crying the whole night if I received news of my father? Later we talked about my panic attack, I was curious to know how it is possible that the loved one of the deceased people gets a panic attack, unhealthy feeling or unstableness during such times even when they are far away. My brother looked at me, smiled and said that it is different with you; this is hardly the second time when you felt uneasy that resulted in mishap. He used to make fun of my anxiety before marriage and rap about it. "Mrs. Anxiety is here, now she will care, more than she bears and make everyone fear. Yo Yo Yo this girl is everywhere, here and there." I knew he did this because of immaturity and his ignorance about the anxiety disorder but he covered his care and fear in his lyrics.

I never told anyone about nights when my imagination left me alone. I felt blank. Those nights I forced myself to think of things that really mattered and realized how far I had come with my fears. My mind would play different tricks and reminds me of my imagination that left and when it would come back. I got no reply, as for those who went with the imagination could not hear me calling and ones who were left with me wondered.

I panicked with such thoughts and gripped the blanket tightly. It feels alive to hold on to something rather than falling totally into such dark memories. My lion's dead, he would not call or signal me that everything was good, I am on my own. As children, we cover ourselves with a blanket when we are scared. I miss being scared of darkness. As an adult, we need dark rooms to fall asleep. We have become the monsters that we were scared off initially. I need to force myself to think pleasant things that was what doctor has advised but my mind takes me to the adventure of the fearful world.

I remember my old habit of thinking something bad would happen to my loved ones. It is there, still. Lost its intensity over time or maybe I lost most of the loved ones. The habit started when I was 17 years old or a bit older. I used to think of all the combinations of misfortune and bad luck happening to family, friends, and relatives. The better part was that it never happened the way I believed it would, but the worse part was that I nevertheless thought about it. Not that I hated them or wished them to suffer but it was the fear of losing them, which caused these thoughts in the first place. Every time when anyone died or if there was any mishap, I observed it happened in a way I did not think about, so, I started believing that if I think about it, it would not happen and divert for now. People have habit of saying, "Never thought I met him for the last time or something so bad will happen to him" but I took the courage of going through it.

When grandmother's report confirmed her illness with cancer, everyone said this one thing common, "How can this happen to you of all people?" Last, when we saw her, she was kicking. She was 78 and people need to say good things upon meeting her. I did not understand and thought I was to be blamed, as I never thought about it. I missed it and then I missed my grandma, forever. Therefore, I took it as a responsibility to think out all the possibilities in order to save everyone I love, but they did not be forceful thoughts. Thoughts had to be natural and the conditions had to be unfortunate.

When grandma was admitted in the hospital and going through treatment, sometimes she got heavy breathing, sometimes unending cough as if she would cough her soul out. At such an old age that must have been very painful, but I never forgot to end her life in my thoughts when she breathed heavily, coughed, had high fever or had a body ache. This way I believed I kept her alive. She passed away while I was sleeping. My eyes opened at 2 AM and found my mother sitting beside me. What cause my eyes to open at that time in the night? It only happened earlier if I wanted to go. Later, I came to know that she did not wake up from her sleep. One of the things that I missed. This was the incident that accelerated my habit of worrying.

The moment my mother went out to the market, rickshaw puller would kidnap her. If the rickshaw puller is from around and we knew him, then my mind will present another possibility or maybe he would turn against us. If father was late from office, someone stabbed him, or he was involved in an accident of some kind. I was so deep inside these thoughts that after a while it felt normal to kill or torture people whom I loved.

At one instant, I even felt proud about it. Mother called my younger brother to enquire when he would be back from his classes. He replied that he was at the Metro station and would be home hardly in half an hour. We waited for an hour, his phone battery was almost dead, a fact that he did not feel important to mention. Mother became anxious so did I. Phone switched off; half an hour became more than an hour. I took the charge and went to my room. Thought hard about all the possibilities that could happen from metro station to home. Accident, kidnapping, stabbing, quarrel, medical needs, girl, boy, and other things possible. One after the other. I was killing him on the street when the doorbell rang, and the boy entered. He said that there was an accident due to that too much traffic and people could not move for almost half an hour. Mother was relieved. That accident he mentioned could have happened with him, I thought. If only I had not thought, it could have been him. I felt proud with an inflated chest. A hero whose mysterious work that could be understood by no one.

The feeling of worry never subsided in me. There were times when I was deep in worry without knowing the reason. I used to haunt reasons. However, after thinking hard and concluding that there is nothing to worry, sometimes I believed that I had forgotten the reason. On the other hand, that it was around for me to figure out and that the sixth sense had alerted me beforehand. I always had feeling to be on alert, even when someone at home is sleeping; I looked at their stomach's movement to make sure that they are resting for time being and not resting in peace.

When nothing bad happened, I lied down happy and successful, but I knew once my guard was down, they would come. I had seen their eyes twinkling at me, monsters of darkness but it never occurred that this was the starting of never-ending torment in my mind and that the time is not under control. I went deeper and deeper and lived more than half of my life in fear. Fear of being alone, fear of losing precious people around me. I thought wouldn't it be better, if everybody dies at once? A painless death, a death that makes everyone's life merrier. However, I read somewhere to be optimistic and being one lead me to feel that I am saving many lives on a daily basis and the success rate was very high, as high as pills in the bottle kept on the side table; touching the cap, my pills of anxiety. I remember taking them after dinner. Nothing works in old age.

I turned towards the right side of the bed and feeling of guilt punched me; I should have sent him a message that I could not come. I should never have made him wait for so long. All the old memories crawled back, all the closed doors were open, and I could feel the past in my present while standing at the River View Side. I saw the world that existed long back but had no future. To face him became more difficult. I rewind a hundred times in my mind, walking to him, asking him, "How has life treated you? How many children do you have? Where are they? What are they up to? What are you up to these days? How many times did you marry?" He will laugh and say nine, one more to go. "Where is that one more to go?" "May be somewhere near me" and we will both laugh. "Did you do those things that you talked about passionately while curling my hair with your fingers?" Should I ask this? This sounds desperate. He may think that am alone and want him badly.

Anyways, when we meet, I will first apologize for not showing up. I will say things like old times. He will listen to them, laugh and think that I remember it all, that I am still fun, not young but fun. I will try to be expressive with my eyes; he always complimented me back then, my two stars. He will say,

"I waited years for you darling, one more day is just fine." I know it is not, but my legs gave up walking in his direction. My knees felt weak. He will understand and shrug it.

Isn't this a miracle to come together? Only if he has not changed, time changes people, it changed me. When we were together, I could never have imagined making him wait, let alone not showing up. I am scared of what we will become of me in such an old age. There is no hope, neither back then nor in the future. We are losers, cursed ones. My heart is thumping. Is this one of those fake heart attacks like symptoms that rockets anxiety level. Should I swallow more pills? I close my eyes, and in the darkness, two dark waves shaped in the form of hands pull me swiftly.

I am ready to meet you the next morning sitting on the bench at the River View Side. The Sun is glowing in front of me. It looks like one of those children's drawings where in, a river is flowing, the sun is fixed between two mountains and birds are gliding randomly, but specifically three to four birds appear to come from the sun and their sharp silhouettes are growing every instant. Happy people are there, and children are playing. I turn towards Poori to grasp the beauty and on the front bench; you are sitting. I wave at you and you look at me. A few more steps and we will meet. No one is to stop us. No one to come between us. You start to walk towards me and with each step of yours, sun pulled below, and river moved away from us. After few of your steps, there was no sun, only shallow reflecting sunshine behind the mountain shaking vigorously. River View Side is almost dark, and you appear as those birds' silhouettes coming towards me. You enter my head, circle around, making me dizzy and I wake up. My eyes are wide open staring at the ceiling like my husband's eyes at his last moment. Is this one of those dreams that gives bad omens?

I slept hardly for two hours. Sound of children coming from downstairs, it is morning. My whole body is aching. I get up to take care of breakfast and get the children ready for school. I put a sweater on and step out of the room. Receiving thundering good morning from kids and a chain of thoughts lined up saying that I am lucky to have this. I cannot ruin this for my own selfish life. What will people say? A 50-year-old woman is having affairs when she has two younger generations that look up to her. What effect will such things bring on to them? With a heavy heart and a fake smile, I walk towards the kitchen.

It hardly takes us half an hour and children are ready with their backpack to leave for school. I request my darling daughter to take them to the bus stop, as I am deprived of good sleep. She gives me a funny look similar to what she gives to children for not listening. Once she is back, she enquires about my health. I disregard her question saying that there is a difference between not being well and not sleeping well and she debated there is not. She asks me to sleep some more but I refuse and sit on the couch.

She gets our breakfast and we switch on the TV. On the channel, they are showing fat burner belts and giving guarantees for results with a fifty percent discount. Well, I can consider getting one I thought, holding handful of tummies and given the situation. "Do you have two stomachs, one for food and another to show off" he used to say. I had a flat stomach, single chin, a visible jaw line and a lustrous hair. Life took them slowly and gave more where less was required. Will he still find me beautiful, wrinkles all over the body and stomach hanging out competing with chest and winning with great margin? My dream of the fat burner belt shattered, as my daughter switched the channel adding that they make fools of us. She preferred news channel that explains about the weather's bad condition. Taking a bite of chapatti dipped in tea, she enquires if I want to watch about fat burner. I plainly dismiss. Sometimes I feel she has a device to read my thoughts. We heard about the weather for the next 5 minutes finishing our breakfast. She took the dishes to the kitchen and I get up to wash my hands. I look for a towel when suddenly there is a change from weather reporting to breaking news; news channels have a separate loud breaking sound for breaking news. I went to the room thinking there is breaking news every hour of the day.

Shutting the door, every hinge supporting it shouts screeching sound, I take the paper out kept under the mattress and lay down. It has his number. Should I ping him now? No, I will ping him after lunch. It should not look desperate. I hear my daughter going up the stairs and count seven thuds that does not equal to 13 stairs. "I jumped a few", she shouts. I reply that I know. Thirteen thuds confirm that she climbs the stairs all right. I lay down hugging 10 digits on the piece of paper and that piece of paper calms me more than popping two pills last night. That piece of paper is hope, hope of happiness. It says that there can be love in my life. There can still be a person in my life who will take care of me, listen to me. People will ask me about him. How much does he care for me? With these happy thoughts, I slept with hope of new beginnings.

Eyelid responded when it felt as if something or someone touched and called me. I get up to check and it is the TV. The breaking news was breaking about Statue killer. Reporter is saying he murdered a man last night and made a statue of him. Well that is what he does; I responded on his face with my tongue out and switched off the TV. My daughter keeps tabs of all the killings, she knows about the areas, victim's name, their background and what not. I do not understand the curiosity of children with such things, I thought going back to the kitchen to cut ladyfingers for lunch. That is what we have in the weekly menu. Kids are very particular about green vegetables in the menu, more than we are.

What must he be doing? Watching the news about the same stupid statue killer, I thought. He must be angry. He has the right to be. I look at the used tea pan in the sink, dirty and dry. "Why you do not put some water in the pan?" he used to say. "It will be easy for you to wash, let me show you." He will pour some water in the pan, and then with a tea strainer filter all the tealeaves and throw it off in the garbage. "See! Easy right? If you do this every time right after making tea, you do not have to put much effort in cleaning tea pans for the next time", he would lecture me, but would never wash the pan himself. He loved tea. At times, I thought more than me. One thought after another one approach me and making it difficult to concentrate on anything. Thoughts are exploding in my mind like lava pushing to come out, slowly damaging the shape of mountain and then everything around it.

The volcanic eruption was paused when my daughter came down running, and I counted only five thuds. I scream, "Do not do that." She replies, "I am fine *maa*." A mother of two jumping like a teenager. Switching on the TV, she announces to the whole house that her friend was right, that the statue killer was done with our area. "Come *maa* let us watch, it happened at River View Side where you went to meet your friend yesterday." I feel a shiver in my spine thinking if it could have been him. I reply that it is nonsense to give so much importance to such a disgraceful thing and that the killer must be enjoying and getting encouragement from all of this. "Okay I can manage to watch alone", she replies.

Anyhow, from then on, I receive all the bullet points showed on TV standing in the kitchen, she made sure of that. "They are saying it happened around 9 PM and it is highly unlikely for anyone to be around in such a cold weather. One of the guys in the panel is politician and he said, people welcome such things on them by being out late at night. Now, all the panel members are shouting at each other. *Maa*, this happened after two hours when you came back from the same place." She said this in a relaxing tone. I switch on the gas stove and put refined oil in the *kadahi*.

"Killer left a note with an important title, but the police are not ready to make it public. They are saying that it is of no importance to common people and that expert opinion is this may help them catch killer as this is the first time, he communicated with them. Almost all the media channels are at the spot and the Poori has boundary of yellow tapes. The police are neither letting anyone near the statue nor answering any questions."

"That is what they do, they hide facts so people cannot raise the right questions and they can keep on dodging", I said.

"Well, they have confirmed he is a male."

My hands stopped, "Is it him? No, it cannot be. God! Please."

"They think he is a male somewhere between 35 and 40", she added.

"Thank God!" I said.

"Why thank god, if he is between 35 and 40."

"Nothing", I said.

"That is weird *maa*!"

"Now they are interviewing the person who saw the statue

and called the police. *Maaaaa!*"

"What happened?" I scream.

"Nothing I thought that if you were the first person that saw the statue, they would have been interviewing you."

I am irritated by her reaction and say, "I could have been the victim as well."

"Do not say all these nonsense things", she said with a discouraging tone.

After a pause, I enquire of my daughter if the jogger had read the note.

"No, he did not go close; instead he called on 100 right away."

"Well, if he had read it, you can go ask the details from him."

"Not funny, *Maa!*"

I put the ladyfingers in the *Kadahi*, set the knob at low and cover it with the lid. This will cook now. I put some water into this dry pan.

"They will be releasing the photo soon. Until now, nobody has filed a complaint of a missing person. He must be staying alone", she added.

How unlucky his family is if he were a family man. In that case, someone would have filed a missing person complaint, or a businessperson on a tour went to relax at the River View Side and his family is thinking he is busy with work. Poor souls did not even know what calamity has fallen on to them. In all of this, the best-case scenario would be a person with no family, all alone, nobody to look after and no one to cry for him. It is still very sad being murdered and to become a statue. How painful would that have been? Nevertheless, in a way, it is a god's favour for the lonely soul. Have I seen his face? There were not many people yesterday.

"When are they going to release his picture?", I asked my live reporter sitting in front of the TV.

"There is no ETA for that, and they will be releasing his morphed photo for public views only in case nobody comes forward as relatives. So, we need to wait and next there will be a panel of experts assessing the whole situation."

"They are no experts", I said.

"Two of them have 20 years of experience and PhD's in this line of work", came the reply.

"Okay, in that case you enjoy their gibberish; I am going to my room."

"Cool, sleep well."

Yea! Experts! To understand a roadside killer, they need 20 years of experience with PhD's. Nice way to live a life. Then I smile thinking what he must be thinking. Is he watching same gibberish or laying down thinking about us? I smile again. I can feel something special knocking that was unknown for so long and rushing throughout my body. I am scared if an old body such as mine can take this nuisance. Can his body do it as well? I smile again!

I slept for almost 3 hours and woke up thinking about ladyfingers. I rushed towards the kitchen and found nothing on the stove, my sweet girl took care of it. My head is hurting bad, this is what happens when you sleep wrong times in day. The pan filled with water was resting in sink. I clean it to make some tea. The TV is still on with low volume and I ask my girl if she would like to have some Tea. She comes running like a baby. The difference today is that she runs to help me and 20 years ago, she ran into my arms.

"Go *maa*, I will make a strong cup of tea."

"It is okay, let me."

"No, you go."

While walking towards the room I thanked her for taking care of the ladyfingers.

She said, "Let us have tea and biscuit in front of the TV, the old songs special is coming on different channel."

"Oh! Okay" and I changed my direction. My legs were aching as if I ran in a marathon instead of sleeping for the last three hours. I thought of running into HIS arms and here I am taking small steps towards the sofa. Making myself comfortable against the cushion, I saw a girl doing belly dance on the TV. I took the remote and changed it to a news channel. The TV screen is split into two parts. The left half of the TV has the anchor and the right half has a blurred pixelated image of a face. Slowly, pixel by pixel it is loading. It is as if someone is erasing a pencil sketch from the paper in square.

"The picture will take at least 5 minutes to render and this image is morphed only so relatives or known people can know about the tragedy and contact the authorities", the anchor said.

I can see a baldhead; at first, they blacked out the upper part.

What all did he use to cure balding?

"Nothing works", he would say after using each of the new products in the market.

"See am losing more hairs than I can grow back. You do not even care for my hair. All you want me to be is to be clean-shaven or to grow a goatee, I will not let your palm slip on my chin anymore and I will grow a beard as well", he used to say.

"What is going on *maa*?" she enquired from the kitchen.

They are displaying victim's face. It will load in another two minutes.

Those two minutes followed by two hours

I come back to my senses after almost two hours. I feel the dryness of tears on my chin and break them into pieces. All I can remember is that something dreadful has happened but cannot recall. One of those feeling when something catastrophic happened but I was unable to recall, something similar has happened last night as well. Was it one of my anxiety attacks? I need to see the doctor. No, I am not sure. My daughter is hugging both of my legs. She is sleeping with her head on my lap. I can feel some wetness on my lap. Did she cry? I hear the sound of an old man on TV. When I take the trouble to look at it, an astrologer is explaining the effect of moon on the mood of the husband. I wanted to wake her up and ask what I did. She is sleeping calmly and waking her up is like waking up half an hour of lecture. The centre table had two cups full of tea and few biscuits on the plate. Whatever happened, happened before she got tea and biscuits, was it? My throat is dry, dry as if an ocean has cried and turned into a desert. It demands fluid. I can taste the ocean on my lips.

To avoid any movements that could wake up my girl, I reach to one of the teacups. I take a big gulp. I do not have the strength and decide to crush the cushion slowly. Trying to find the pieces of lost time and caressing her head, I move into the purgatory of sleep and wake up when I feel lightness on my leg. This time she is staring right on my face to as if she is trying to find me but with patience, care and fear.

"Everything all right, my child?"

"Yes, *maa*. What had happened to you?" she asks politely. "I got so worried, you were crying. No, howling. When I came back with the tea, you were covering your face with the dupatta. I tried asking many times what happened, but you kept on like that. When I removed your hand, you started crying and then howled. I have never seen you like that. I got scared *maa*. What did you see? Why you were saying repeatedly that you wanted to go to River View Side and that he is still waiting. Who is waiting? *Maa*, do not cry again, please. Tell me what is wrong?"

The dryness on my face is gone. Two women are crying, the first one knew the reason and the second one knew the first one. The first one pleaded the man for an apology and the second one pleaded the first one to stop crying.

"How could I beta?" A man died for me for the second time. All he did was wait for me and I did not have the courage to walk up to him. I got scared beta, to stand in front of my past and an unknown future. An unknown future, a happy future. Who wants to run away from a happy future? I did, as if I could not accept a happy version of myself. Why does it always happen to me? Why did I not have the courage to walk up to my happiness? Nobody was there to stop me. Parents, society and not even your dad. This was the second chance to right the wrong. When I was with him, everything felt special. Now that there was the slightest chance of him being back in my life…

After five minutes, I open my eyes in my daughter's lap.

"Everything will be all right; you take rest. The children will be here soon from the school", she said.

"I feel embarrassed and request her to take me to my room please; I do not want them to see me like this."

I fell asleep as soon as I was on the bed and woke up to the sound of the children entering the house. Laying down on the bed, I thought that this day is the worst day of my life and every second of it is building guilt inside me. I wanted to see him for the last time; all I have of his, is his number and that is of no use now. I get up, take a bottle of water from kitchen, and switch on the news channel to watch who is there to take care of his body and where the cremation would take place.

After all the blabbering of the news anchor, a detailed report was given on the incident. The Statue killer committed the murder; the body cannot be moved until tomorrow morning as directed by the killer. He seemed to have used some chemicals that need to vaporize before moving the body. This was another heart wrenching part. In such a cold weather, the body will freeze in a couple of hours. How will the fluid vaporize? This might be another one of the killer's ways to be in the lime light, he is stretching. The police will be on the rounds the whole night. My daughter joins me and upon enquiring about the children, she confirms that they are sleeping. She has many questions on her face. Each word that she is uttering and my acknowledgement towards her is giving her the strength to ask the right questions. So, before she asked something more, I tell her, "Not today. Some other day."

But she knew now that he was the guy whom I went to meet and did not meet. I watched all the details given on the news keenly and decided that today I would meet him. I will walk up to him and sit next to him until and unless my guilt and sorrow turns into some other emotion.

Once it was dark enough and my daughter was busy with children, I said that I needed a walk to calm my nerves. She looks at me and counts the number of layers of clothes that I am wearing. Inner, overcoat, cap and muffler. She makes me wear the thin jacket inside the over coat, hugs me tight and asks me to return soon. I say that I will be back as there is nowhere else, I can go. As today is the day I cried, she let it pass. Else, she would have said, "No need to act like an unsupported old woman. You are our world."

I step out.

CHAPTER 11

HIS

Still hopeless, sitting in front of the departmental store, an old couple walks by and that reminds me I am dead. I could not have a life like theirs. I am all over the news, and the way the coverage is done, I feel it would take a while for them to lose me from the news channel. The media channel should be sensitive about such issues I was just thinking that this morning. Now I am the news. Lucky me. My body needs to be unmoved until tomorrow, must be life and death.

I have thought hundreds of times about the probability of her coming this way; eventually it is going to be zero. If she knew about me by now, she would not be in a condition to leave the house and come to the departmental store for shopping vegetables. At least I am sure about that, so, why did I choose this place then. Why am I so dumb even after dying? If she does not know about me, she might come this way. She may try calling on my number, but I cannot go back. Who knows if Death's mood is changed and she would no longer let me lose like this? Mrs. Death might be waiting or working on someone else at this moment and each second, I feel she can call upon me, anytime.

Anyways If I would have found her, I could have seen her crying; taking turns in her bed remembering me. I would have seen how she is living her life. I don't know but it feels very important to find out where she lives, how does her room look like? How does she smell? How big is her house? How cleanly does she manage everything? Who all are staying with her? I could have slept next to her on her bed. How would that feel? I want to find out, if she is lonely or she has a happy life going on. Her happy life would have assured me that all is well, and she is in happy states. If she is sad and lonely that would have assured me that, we are on the same level of life. Why am I thinking in this way about her? Why in a single day without knowing how she lived her life am I worried about her wellbeing? Love that had died long back, resurrected strongly in me. To look at this differently, if we had not met then there would have been no chance of me visiting River View Side in such a cold weather. Mostly my days would have passed in my room with a heat blower, a cup of tea and a book, implying that I would have been alive and alone.

With a heavy soul, I start to walk in the direction of River View Side. To hell with everyone, I am dead and that matters more than all the other things. Where would I go after this? What would happen to me? My body must have started decomposing but it will take time because of the cold weather. When I almost reach the River View Side, I take a turn towards the Coffee Stall to kill time. Yes, I thought I had a lot of it. There was a *police wala* sipping hot coffee, listening to the Coffee Stall owner's lecture about the area and how much development it needed. Next, to the coffee stall is a heavy built woman having Maggie and coffee. She is eating with a great dedication. Taking a deep breath, the *police wala* says that the people of this area is safe, but the police failed the man who lost his life.

"Why don't we have more security?" demanded the coffee stall owner while passing biscuits in direction of another cop.

"The whole department who is working to catch killer has been shifted immediately to another area that is most likely to be hit. Now, there will be even less security. Think about it like this. In this whole area, that is spread around 2 kilometres and that has a boundary of only half a kilometre, only two of us are posted. We asked this to our boss, and he said that the killer is done with our area. Now, there will be no one in such a cold weather."

Hearing the last statement, the coffee stall owner rolled his eyes towards the woman sitting and sipping coffee. All four of us focused on her and one of the police said in a harsh tone, "Madam, it is not allowed to be near River View Side for two days, there is a dead body sitting on the bench and who knows killer can be still around."

She replies, "Okay", pull out the wallet from her breast pocket, and pays. Least interested in making conversation, she leaves. The Coffee stall owner says that she lost her husband a few days back. She comes daily and spends a lot of time here. Hearing this annoys one of the *police wala* and he says, "Should we do our job or think of every serious matter personally and let the rules be unfollowed?"

After gulping the whole cup, both of the *police wala's* left in the opposite direction to the River View Side. The coffee stall owner said that it is the wrong direction, upon which both reply, "Do your work or wind up and go home."

I think about my body left alone on the bench, sitting like one of those mummies that I watched on the discovery channel. The Coffee stall owner seems to be scared by the fact that he is alone with a dead body just 500 m away from him by the cops, so, he winds up and left.

Annoyed sitting alone, I decide to walk up to Poori Mountain and ask Mrs. Death a relevant question about what would happen to me from now on. Once the Poori Mountain is in sight, I see a manly figure standing in front of me. I mean my dead body. Is the killer back but the figure is bigger compared to the killer? I am trying to process if that guy is one of the cops, but he is dangerously closed to me against the guidelines. Suddenly, a figure passes next to me. Overcoat, cap and muffler. Since when women are assigned duty around a dead body with a man. She paced up and I followed her. When we reached near to Poori Mountain, she stops, and I look up standing behind her. The figure standing in front of my dead body was I. The woman I followed covered her face with both of her hands. In the next instant, she shrugged and started walking. I could not move, no, this should not be happening, manly walk, you fool, and you should not have come.

"You should not see me like this, dead and decomposed."

I shout to go back, she cannot hear me. I run before her, throw my hands to stop and embrace her. No one can stop this woman once you look at her face, rage mixed with love more powerful than the mother of all bombs.

There is a woman and three of me present on top of Poori Mountain. One dead body sitting in a relaxed pose, Mrs. Death wearing my face and winking me for the fourth time, I am standing next to my dead body and a woman crying on the bench. Three of me surrounds one of her. If only she knew.

I want to console her, sit next to her between my dead body and her but Mrs. Death's presence made everything awkward. On top of it her continuous winking and also, I do not want to see myself eye to eye.

I want to know what she is thinking. She has stopped crying and is looking towards the unending frozen white crap. If I could kiss the warmth of her hand, then this moment would have become the most beautiful moment of my life or death even with my dead body sitting next.

All three of me felt a breach of privacy when a figure jumped up the stairs and within seconds reached her. When he pulled back his hand, I saw the same hellhound. By the time, I understood why Mrs. Death was wearing me; she, my man, my woman, was unconscious on the bench. I turn towards Mrs. Death and she winks again. Everything is blurred and fuzzy.

ACKNOWLEDGEMENTS

I would like to thank my parents and sisters for making me who I am today.

A very special thanks to Suhail A Mulla for being an early draft reader, editor and for being a serious contributor throughout the development of the book.

Thank you to Priti Kumari, Sohaib Zaman and Ysabel Caballes for being trusted early readers. Your suggestions meant a lot.

And a very special thanks to the Leadstart Publication team, Malini Nair and book editor Abhishek James Chandran for all the work we put as a team.

A big thank you to Md. Adil Ashraf and all those unnamed people that have been always supportive and encouraging of my endeavors.

I am very grateful to the Almighty Allah for helping me throughout this journey.

ABOUT THE AUTHOR

Saad Quadri is a working professional with more than half a decade of experience in the Indian IT industry. Being from an academic background of Electronics and Communications Engineering from the famed Visvesvaraya Technological University, he turned to writing when he discovered that he had a lot to say and no outlet to say those things.

Hailing from Gaya in Bihar but having travelled a fair distance in India (for education and work), he has had the opportunity to meet people from different backgrounds and sensibilities around the country.

When he is not contemplating the plot of his next book, he can be found winning in Carrom, adjusting the gutting on his Badminton racket, organizing LAN parties to play multiplayer games with friends, reading any book that he gets his hands on and binging on Netflix.

These days, he lives in Bangalore where he works in Business Intelligence. But his favourite job is telling stories with his writing.

www.ingramcontent.com/pod-product-compliance
Lightning Source LLC
LaVergne TN
LVHW051535170726
843492LV00006B/1776